A Wild Mother Goose Chase

a murder mystery novel by

Tricia Mack

ISBN: 979-8-218-29594-3

This is a work of fiction. Names, characters, places, and incidents either are a product of the author's imagination or are used fictitiously. Any resemblance to actual persons, living or dead, events, or locales is entirely coincidental.

Dedicated to my husband and daughter who inspire me every day.

CHAPTER ONE

"Please share!" a slightly disheveled, young mom pleaded with her one-and-a-half-year-old daughter, Lilly, as they played tug-of-war with a library book. "It's time to give it back and let someone else read it. Why don't we let go of this book, so we can trade it in for some new ones, okay?" The two made their way through the entrance of the community library, pushing open a heavy wooden door.

As soon as they walked inside, Lilly happily dropped the book and pranced into the otherwise quiet room, singing loudly the first three words of *Titsy Titsy Sider* over and over again. A man sitting at an outdated library computer glanced judgingly over the monitor toward mother and daughter. Luckily, the kids' corner soon piqued Lilly's interest, which allowed for a reprieve from her song. Little did that gentleman know but *Titsy Titsy Sider* had been going on since the moment Lilly was clicked into her car-seat and the whole ride over.

"Hello, Hen," the librarian called, popping up from behind the long counter desk.

"Sorry." Hen glanced over at Lilly happily flipping through board books.

"Are you kidding? We love our young readers!" The librarian's eyes darted to judgmental computer man, and he quickly turned his gaze back to the screen.

"Thanks" Hen said with a smile, placing a large stack of children's books on the counter. "Speaking of that, Lilly is just loving books lately! She likes any kind of stories really, but especially those nursery rhyme books you suggested. She gobbles them up." Hen paused and clarified, "I mean, not literally. My child isn't eating your books."

The librarian laughed, "I figured. I won't tell if I find a few bite marks though."

Hen smiled again, relieved to be in one of the very few places where she felt like she and Lilly were actually welcome. It's amazing how inaccessible the world suddenly seems once you have a baby, and double that with a toddler.

She took a moment to renew the book she was reading…again. *It's hard to have any time to shower, let alone read for fun*, Hen thought to herself in an attempt to excuse her inability to finish anything. Her eyes darted to the book, hoping that the librarian wouldn't see Hen's old business card shoved into its pages and wouldn't notice the fact that her makeshift bookmark was in almost the exact same spot as it had been last time she renewed it. *This librarian sees a million books a day. I'm sure she doesn't remember,* Hen's inner voice assured her.

Hen glanced back to the kids' corner, content to see Lilly sitting quietly, but as she made her way around a tall bookshelf, she nearly jumped out of her skin. Lilly wasn't alone. An elderly woman was plunked down in the often-empty rocking chair in the corner of the kids' section.

Hen must have appeared startled because the woman immediately reassured her, "Don't worry, Mom. We were just reading a story. I love to see young ones so excited about books." The old woman's smile seemed genuine, though Hen made a point to not leave her daughter's side until they were home.

"It's okay." Hen sat beside her daughter and listened to the kindly, old woman as she read aloud the rest of the story. She was an engaging narrator, giving each character his own voice. Lilly was enthralled. Come to think of it, so was Hen. By the end of the tale, the old woman seemingly lost in thought muttered, "All stories teach us lessons, but nursery rhymes, they ring with truths."

"Oh, Lilly loves nursery rhymes," Hen blurted out. This definitely piqued the interest of the old woman, her eyes sparkling. However, Lilly's attention span was spent, and she was off pulling out toys from under the train table. As she played, Hen and the old woman chatted briefly until their conversation was interrupted by a large man in an even larger suit. Hen recognized him as the man at the computer.

"We have to go," he scolded.

"I know, I know," the old woman replied. She turned to Hen. "Nice to have met you, dear." Her eyes lingered longer than Hen expected, making her feel a bit uncomfortable.

"Same here."

As the woman was hastily escorted out of the library by her companion, Hen turned her attention back to Lilly playing take-out-every-toy-and-put-it-on-the-floor, a game she loved playing at home as well.

"Alright Lilly, time to clean up," Hen said as cheerfully as she could, awaiting the meltdown.

"Keen up, keen up!" Lilly sang, throwing the toys back in the bin. Hen leaned down and gave her a big kiss on the head. Lilly really was full of surprises sometimes.

The two made their way home with another handful of books checked out for Lilly, which Hen had promptly placed into her reusable green bag.

After dinner and bath and tooth-brushing and story time, Lilly was fast asleep, and Hen had a moment to think and reflect. *It had been a long day, but a good one,* she thought. She collapsed on her bed, pulling the covers over her.

This was the time of day that was quiet. In these moments, there was a palpable emptiness that, against her best efforts, would fill with loneliness. Sleeping alone never bothered her before, but after a long day of motherhood, it was exceptionally… lonely.

It wasn't like Harry was dead or anything dramatic like that. He was just away on business, again. This time he had said it would be about a month. Shorter than last time. Hen wanted to be supportive, wanted to champion his goals and dreams, but she also wanted to cry like Lilly and plead for him to stay. The latter never won out. Hen was nothing if not a supportive wife, most of the time to her own detriment.

She reached out to the bedside table for her library book, but it wasn't there. *Go figure.* Hen was too exhausted to run downstairs and probably also too much so to even remember anything that she'd read anyway. Her memory was shot.

In the quietness of the night, Hen's thoughts were of her daughter, her distant husband, and for a fleeting moment, that odd interaction with the woman in the rocking chair. Hen had no way of knowing at the time, but her brief encounter with that strange yet engaging woman would forever alter Henrietta Bellemore's life.

CHAPTER TWO

3 weeks later

"That's encouraging," Hen said halfheartedly, gritting her teeth and forcing a smile. Harry couldn't see her through the phone, but she hoped to make her tone as believable as possible.

"I know!" he retorted. He had definitely not picked up on the strain in her voice. Hen found herself thinking the sarcastic responses she would never actually say. Harry continued, "I really am learning so much." *Uh huh. You say that every time you leave for these all-too-frequent business trips.* "I've never been so busy though!" *YOU'VE been busy? I bet you at least have time to use the bathroom.* "You wouldn't believe how much work it is, keeping up with these guys." *Try keeping up with your daughter.*

Pause.

"Thank you for supporting me in this," Harry said softly. Hen held the phone away from her face feeling a pang of guilt for her inner thoughts. She released a sigh and a tear trickled down her face. She brought the phone back to her ear.

"Of course."

Harry had just informed his wife that he was staying away a bit longer and had been asked to fill a temporary role in the company for a few weeks. A great opportunity to get his foot in the door, he had said. As she hung up the phone, Hen's heart sank. *Just another few weeks more,* she assured herself. She literally shook her head to reset her thoughts and move on.

Hen's gaze went to the video baby monitor. *How is she so beautiful?* she thought looking at sweet little Lilly napping peacefully in her crib. Grabbing her now-cold coffee, Hen stepped out onto the porch to enjoy the late morning sun and check the mailbox.

"Geez!" she said aloud, then covered her mouth as to not wake the sleeping baby down the hall.

The porch was filled with boxes. Hen never ordered anything. Okay, usually never. (There was that one time she had drank a rare bottle of wine after putting Lilly to bed and had tipsily purchased an iguana shaped oven mitt… which never did arrive, come to think of it.) Needless to say, her porch had never seen so many packages at once.

Upon closer inspection, she noticed that the boxes were all unmarked. *This had to have been a mistake.*

She grabbed the stack of mail out of the box and sat down with her cold mug. Bill. Credit-card offer. Credit-card offer. Credit-card offer. *Every credit-card company in the world must have our name and address!* Thank you card from her cousin's wedding shower. *She is so on the ball.* Hen hated writing thank you cards. *Why the formality? I know you're thankful. You said thank you when you got the gift. Save yourself the postage. Cute stationery though.* Magazine. Coupons. A new flyer for the pizza shop around the corner. *Save that.* And a tiny envelope. It was yellowed around the edges as if it had been printed in the 50s and stashed away in a cupboard collecting dust and mold. Come to think of it, it even smelled a little moldy.

A delicate little card was inside. The cover displayed an illustration of a goose in a bonnet. Inside, in loopy calligraphy, it read:

Henrietta,
Hope you girls find the truths in these books.
Talk to you soon,
Mrs. Nettles

Books? Hen pulled up the tape off of one of the boxes. They were indeed filled with children's books. No mistaking that these packages were meant for her. But who is Mrs. Nettles? The name didn't ring a bell. She must have sent at least twenty books, maybe more. Surely, she was a relative or something cleaning out her attic.

Old people like to do that, clean out their stuff and guilt younger generations to take the things they don't want anymore. It's actually kind of brilliant, one less trip to the thrift store. A few months prior, Hen had received a giant ceramic heron, as in the fish-eating bird, from her Aunt Gwenith which she reluctantly placed in her front garden. Unfortunately, Lilly soon grew an attachment to the ugly old thing and Hen's hopes to get rid of it were dashed.

Hen sighed. *Guess I need to write a thank you card.*

After shoving the boxes into the spare room, Hen scribbled a half-hearted "Thank you so much! Lilly will love these!" and signed her name, tucking the generic card into its envelope. But what was Mrs. Nettles' address? None of the packages had a return address, not even the card itself.

Before she had another moment to think on it, Lilly was awake and wiggling around in her crib on the monitor. Hen made her way to the nursery, snack in hand, and got in a little cuddle time with Lilly.

As the day went on, she texted her mom, her aunt, and even her snobby sister-in-law "Any idea who Mrs. Nettles is?" but by the evening, she had come up empty. There was no Mrs. Nettles in her family.

Hen distractedly went through the nighttime routine with Lilly and once she was fast asleep, slumped down on the sofa. *Okay. Time to get my mind off of Mrs. Nettles and all those books I have to find a place for. I'm going to actually read that novel from the library.* She dug through her green bag to no avail. *Where the heck is it?* Defeated, Hen pulled out the local magazine from the stack of mail determined to spend her few quiet hours reading rather than just zoning out in front of the television.

The front cover was a clean-shaven man with a very large, very white smile. "Giving Back: Derrick Tittle's Foundation of Inspiration" it read below his beaming face. Hen flipped through the story about Mr. Tittle and his "zest for helping others". With a local event coming up this weekend, his public relations team was at the top of its game. Everyone seemed to love this man. Funny though, the article didn't say much about the foundation, just about Mr. Tittle himself.

Bing. Hen's phone went off beside her.

Harry's sister, Jackie, had finally texted her back:

"Hey, are you sure it was 'Nettles' N-E-T-T-L-E-S?" *Not sure why she felt the need to spell it out. It's a text. It's already spelled out.* Hen always got the feeling that Jackie considered her an idiot. Times like these were proof and point.

"Yeah, why?" Hen texted back, ignoring the condescension.

"Like Mrs. Nettles and the missing Nettles' fortune?"

"I don't even know what that is."

"Seriously?! It's all over the local news, Hen." Jackie responded, linking an article.

Okay, so I don't want to spend what little downtime I have watching the local news. Geez.

"What We Know About the Nettles Estate" the article read. Hen skimmed through. "Over a million dollars was said to be stashed away in the underground safe beneath the Nettles Mansion, but when the vault was finally opened, it was completely barren. The late Essie Nettles had been found dead in her sleep of natural causes by her visiting physician. At 94, she was the last remaining inhabitant of the Nettles Mansion and the last in the long line of a prominent family. Several of the heirs mentioned in Mrs. Nettles' will are heartbroken and confused. Police are investigating the theft..." The article continued, but Hen saw something that forced her to stop reading.

The article displayed a portrait of the late Mrs. Nettles. Hen almost dropped her phone. The old woman from the library! She was considerably younger in the picture, but it was her, no mistaking. Those dark, piercing eyes, the kindly smirk, the eccentric fashion sense.

She searched frantically for Mrs. Nettles' card. "Talk to you soon," it had read. A lump formed in Hen's throat. *I guess not.*

Out of respect for the deceased, Hen went straight to work putting away the books that had cluttered up her porch that morning. She felt a little guilty about how she had begrudgingly received them. They really were beautiful old books, once she wiped off the dust. They were a bit worse for wear with ink marks on some of the pages but filled with the kinds of intricate illustrations that you just don't find anymore. She found them a place to live in the spare room.

Feeling a little less guilty, Hen threw the boxes in recycling and jumped in the shower to wash off the dust and ick that had somehow transferred from the books to herself. As the warm water ran over her head, a chill ran down her spine. *How did Mrs. Nettles know where she lived?*

The next morning, Hen found herself awake before dawn, and what's more, before Lilly. That almost never happened. She opened her laptop and set down with a (hot!) cup of coffee. Now she was invested. Her morning hours were filled with answering the question: who was Mrs. Nettles?

A socialite and rebel of her time, having kept her maiden name post-marriage, Essie Nettles was the talk of many in her day. She was an actress on the stage but aspired to be a costume designer, sometimes surprising the director when she walked out onstage in her own creations instead of those created and approved for her. She was athletic. Black and white photos showed her in old-timey swimwear and what was considered activewear back in the day. One picture showed her in a long wool skirt with hiking gear in hand. *Highly impractical.* There was an abundance of information about young Essie but very little about old Essie. A number of years ago, after the disappearance of her first and only husband, she became a recluse, hardly ever leaving the decaying Nettles Mansion. *Sad.* She was painted as an eccentric and it seemed as though she was in poor mental health late in her life. *Wow. I didn't notice that at all. She certainly fooled me into thinking she was all there. But, of course, she was an actress and I'm no doctor. What do I know?*

Hen saw the mailman out of the corner of her eye. She lunged at the door and opened it as softly as she could, taking the mail by hand so that the carrier wouldn't slam the box shut and wake up Lilly *like he always did.*

A small, yellowed envelope lay right at the top of the stack. Hen practically threw the other pieces of mail on the table as she ripped it open.

This time, it was an illustration of three fat pigs. She flipped to the contents:

Henrietta,

You have probably realized by now that I am dead.

Wait. What?! Hen had goosebumps all over but started again and continued reading:

Henrietta,

You have probably realized by now that I am dead. I hope your daughter has been enjoying the stories I sent. Nursery rhymes teach us life's lessons, you know. I am writing to request your help. I'll just get to the point so there can be no uncertainty, I have been murdered. Seeing as there is little I can do now to bring forth justice, I leave it to you.

In humble thanks,

Mrs. Nettles

Hen staggered to the couch, flopping herself down in dismay. She had just received a letter from a dead woman.

CHAPTER THREE

If there ever was a supportive friend, it was Abigail Redburn. She was what some may politely call a free spirit, though she was the type who didn't really care what people called her polite or otherwise. Nonetheless, she was the best and most loyal friend Hen had ever known. Hen had been devastated when she moved to the other side of the country a few years ago. Thank goodness for video chat.

"Jealous!" Abby nearly shouted into the phone. "I still have that old Ouija board that I bought when I thought there were ghosts living in our old apartment. Do you remember that? Not so much as a 'hello'. I was using it as a cutting board for a while when I first moved here and didn't have anything for the kitchen. Hope that doesn't come back to haunt me.... Ha!"

"Seriously, Abby. I'm kind of scared. I mean, should I call the police?"

Abby's tone softened, "Well, what is your heart telling you to do?"

"Honestly, I don't know." In anyone else's voice, asking what her heart is saying would seem corny, but somehow Abby gave the words an authenticity. Hen continued, "I mean, she asked me for help. From the grave. Me! Why would she ask *me*?"

"Well, because you're clever and empathetic and are the type of person who would actually consider helping a dead woman you didn't even know. At least enough to call your best friend and talk to her about it."

"But that's the thing. I don't know her, and what's more, she doesn't…didn't…know me either. I mean, I don't even know how she got my address."

"Honestly, I wouldn't worry too much about that part. I mean, she's dead. She's not coming after you. Let's just figure it out. You said you talked to her at the library?"

"Yeah, but just for a minute. It's not like I told her where I live."

"Did you tell her your name?"

"Uh… maybe?"

"Come on, Henny!" Abby was the only person Hen allowed to call her Henny. "Help a girl out! Also, she called you by your full first name. That's weird. No one calls you Henrietta."

"Argh, mom-brain! I can't remember hardly anything we talked about."

"Okay, did she see a piece of mail you had with you or something?"

Pause. A light bulb went off in Hen's head.

"The book," Hen muttered.

"Okay, you're going to need to expand on that. This lady gave you like a hundred books. Which one?"

"No, no." Hen shook her head. "The library book that I had checked out for me. I can't find it anywhere. She must have swiped it from me when we were at the library. It had one of my old business cards from when I tried to sell that skin care line in it. I was using it as a bookmark."

"I told you that was a pyramid sch…"

"I know! I know. I still have a crate of facemasks in the garage!" Hen took a deep breath. "The point is, it had my address on it. And my name. My full name."

"Eureka!" *Only Abby could say things like 'Eureka' in conversation and not sound totally ridiculous.* "Wow, she is sneaky."

"Was. She's dead, remember."

"Right, was… But what if she's not dead? What if she, like, faked her own death?"

"But why?"

Pause. "You've got me there, Henny."

"I really think I should tell someone."

"Okay, decision made!" Abby affirmed. "But maybe just be careful about what you say or at least how you say it. You don't really want people thinking that you're tied to a murder in some way."

"I don't even know if it really was a murder. Maybe she was just crazy."

"True. She doesn't have a great track record here. Sending a stranger a bunch of moldy books and writing her secret messages postmortem."

Hen chuckled, "Yeah. Hey, thanks for always having my back. I'll be glad to tell someone and get this whole thing off my mind. I've got enough on my plate as it is."

"You know I always do. But I still think you should tell Harry. I know I would want to hear about if my spouse was dealing with a crazy old dead lady wanting to avenge her death."

"No, he's busy with his own stuff. I don't want to worry him."

"Okay, but…"

"Hey, I've got to go get lunch ready for Lilly and wake her up."

Abby could see that Hen wasn't in the mood to talk about Harry. "Love her," she said.

"Me too," Hen said back.

"Okay, well keep me posted."

"Will do... Wait, you didn't actually use your Ouija board as a cutting board, right?"

"Love you, Henny," Abby said with a smile and hung up.

After Lilly's lunch of veggie nuggets, grapes, and apple juice and Hen's lunch of left-over veggie nuggets, grapes and one of the secret cookies that she had hidden on the top shelf, the two girls started to get packed into the car to drive to the local station. Hen figured that it would make her seem less crazy to have the notecards in hand when she talked to the police about the whole Mrs. Nettles situation.

Diapers? Check. Lilly's snacks? Check. Binky? Check. Sippy cup of juice for the road? Check. Is Lilly wearing shoes? ...Partial check.

"Where's your other shoe, Silly Lilly?"

"Eeeeee!" Lilly squealed and ran under the table.

"Careful, babe, watch your he-" Thonk.

"Wahhh!" Lilly's playful giggles were immediately replaced with tears as she ran over to Hen while pointing to her forehead, sobbing.

Hen wrapped her arms around her daughter and breathed in deeply. "I'm sorry you bumped your head, baby. It will feel better soon." Hen rubbed her back and after a minute or so Lilly was back to being Lilly. Eventually, Hen found the other tiny, pink sneaker on the bathroom rug. Finally, they were dressed, ready, and out the door. So much preparation for a fifteen-minute drive.

Pulling into the parking lot, Hen could hardly find a spot. She had to cram her minivan into the literal furthest spot from the station. *What is going on?*

After wrangling Lilly out of her car-seat, they pushed through a sea of people standing in the parking lot. Hen looked around. They all looked fairly happy, smiles on faces, gabbing about this and that. *So, not a hostile situation,* she thought, loosening her grip on the toddler in her arms just a bit.

Two men were putting up a banner in front of the community center building. "How Far Will You Go to Inspire?", it read. *A little corny.* Then it came to her. *That's right! That philanthropist guy is holding an event this weekend. Oh my gosh, is it the weekend already? I was going to take Lilly to the park later. It's going to be so busy on a Saturday. Maybe we should just go grocery shopping instead. Poor Lilly, that's so boring...*

A familiar face pulled Hen from the rabbit hole of her own brain.

"Thad?"

Thad Neilson. Hen knew him from middle school. He cheated off of her Spanish tests. Then made her feel like a dork for setting up a folder barrier to stop him from cheating off of her Spanish tests. And then he proceeded to cheat off of her again when she took the folders down after other kids started teasing her about it. Actually, Thad was kind of a jerk in middle school. He was nicer as an adult, or at least he seemed as much.

"Hey! Henrietta Swanson!"

"It's Bellemore now." Hen surprised herself at how quickly she felt the need to correct him.

"Right! Bellemore. That fits you."

"Yeah, I guess so"

20

"And this one's yours?" he asked, gesturing at Lilly who was now burying her face into Hen's chest.

"Yep. This is Lilly." After a few more pleasantries, Hen briefly explained that she "might have some information that the police might find pertinent to an investigation." *The perfect amount of vagueness.*

"Whoa. Which investigation?"

"The Nettles Case." *Ugh. Nice going, Hen.* She was still working on not being an over-sharer when in the presence of other adults.

Thad pried slightly, but Hen changed the subject until it his interest seemed to wane. Just before heading over to the community center next-door, Thad pointed Hen in the direction of the front desk.

"Just make sure you have something to back you up. I think they're sick of hearing about that whole Nettles charade, you know?"

Hen was taken aback a bit. She hadn't even considered that she might need to prove something. *Well, I have the letters, don't I?*

As she walked up to a fidgety woman sitting behind a pane of thick glass, Hen started to feel a little uneasy. *Have I ever even been inside a police station before? I hope they won't think I'm just wasting their time.*

"Can I help you?"

"Um, yes. I have, uh, evidence… er, I mean, information about an investigation." *Why do I sound like the seventh grader who set up folder forts during Spanish tests all of a sudden? Stupid Thad.* She didn't know how it was his fault that she sounded like an idiot, but she was blaming it on him anyway.

There was a long pause while the woman went to grab a piece of paper. *A form of some kind?* The silence was killing her.

"It's about Mrs. Nettles. I have evidence that indicates that there may have been foul play involved." *Oh my god, Hen! Shut up! Don't tell HER that!*

The receptionist stopped searching for whatever it was she had been looking for.

"Ma'am, what is it that you have?" *Crap. Okay, just show her the letters.*

"These…" Hen squeaked out meekly. *Lilly could have done this better.* Hen rooted around in her purse for the little yellowed envelopes.

Nothing.

Her face burning with embarrassment, she put Lilly down and started rooting through the diaper bag.

Nothing.

Double crap. I must have left them at home.

Lilly, catching a glimpse of the graham crackers that Hen had sneakily packed in the diaper bag earlier for a snack at the park, lunged forward. Without thinking, Hen snatched them from her hand. That was it. Lilly started having a full, on the ground, kicking and screaming meltdown. *Triple crap.*

"I'll just come back."

"Mmm-hmm," the receptionist grunted.

Hen picked up the full contents of her purse and diaper bag that was strewn about the floor, her screaming child, and what was left of her dignity and walked out.

CHAPTER FOUR

This particular park was actually pretty quiet for a Saturday. Hen had searched her phone in the police station parking lot for a park she and Lilly hadn't visited before, one that allowed for a good twenty-minute drive for Lilly to doze off and Hen to shake off the awkwardness of her encounter with the receptionist.

The little kid's area was actually fenced in. Hen would have to remember this place. What's more, for a place made for kids to get their crazy out, it was also incredibly beautiful. The breeze wafted scents of blossoms. It was tricky to tell which flowers were giving off the aroma for the sheer number of varieties popping up over the landscape around the park.

Hen parked herself on a bench and gave Lilly a bit of freedom to explore on her own. Enjoying a moment of stillness in her natural surroundings allowed Hen to think on her situation.

Why had the receptionist seemed so disinterested in hearing more about the Nettles case? Maybe Hen really should leave well enough alone. A sick old woman, dealing with the finality of life... maybe she just wanted to play one last character. Hen liked that idea. It made sense. But why was it that she picked Hen (and Lilly) to be her final audience? *Maybe she just liked kids. She took a shine to Lilly anyway.*

Satisfied with her theory, Hen decided to let the authorities take care of it. It was unlikely that she would hear from Mrs. Nettles again anyway, since her second card omitted the 'talk to you soon' sign off included in the first. Hen was definitely the furthest thing from an expert on murder anyway. She would just hinder what already seemed like a convoluted investigation.

"Decision made," Hen said to herself aloud, trying to evoke the confidence of her best friend, Abby. She would just let it alone.

The weight of Mrs. Nettles' entreaty lifted from her shoulders, Hen nearly jumped off the bench to join Lilly as she toddled through a long plastic tube shaped like a hollowed-out log. Hen scooped her up and held her belly-down shouting "Airplane!" as she ran around the park. The little airplane herself couldn't contain her squeals and giggles.

It was nearly dinner time when the girls finally left the park. Hen was decidedly not in the mood for cooking that night and picked up fast food chicken nuggets on the way home instead. *It's been a long day,* she justified to herself. Lilly, having had what a one-and-a-half-year-old might consider the best day ever, was happy as a lark during bath-time, tooth-brushing, and her whole bedtime routine.

Hen put Lilly on her lap, wrapped her in a blanket, and retrieved a library book from the green bag sitting beside her.

"No," Lilly said softly, shaking her head. Hen was surprised. This was usually Lilly's favorite part of bedtime.

"You don't want to read a book?"

"Book!" Lilly replied excitedly.

"Okay, I thought so." Hen opened the library book, but Lilly gently pushed it shut.

"No," she said again.

"I don't know what you want here, babe," Hen responded tenderly.

Lilly slid off her lap and onto the floor, toddling out of the room.

"Where are you going, Silly Lilly?" Hen followed her down the hall and into the spare room. There she stood pointing up at Mrs. Nettles' books that Hen had stacked up on her small corner desk.

"Oh!" Hen finally understood. "Are you sure you want to read one of these and not one of the totally awesome books that we have in your room that weren't sent to us by dead people?"

Lilly excitedly nodded her head yes, not picking up on her mother's sarcasm.

"Okay, okay." Hen handed the book on top to Lilly and walked her back to the rocking chair. They cuddled up to read, but Lilly had a death grip on the old book.

"Please share, Lilly. Let's read it together, okay?" Hen asked softly. Lilly let loose her grasp and Hen cracked open the old book's delicate spine.

"A was an Apple Pie," she read. Hen remembered this old nursery rhyme. It started out with normal things one would do to an apple pie, "B bit it. C cut it," but then it got a little weird, "J joined it." *What does that even mean? Couldn't J 'jab' at it or 'jam' his finger in it or 'jiggle' it or something?* Hen laughed at her own inner thoughts. Lilly looked up at her impatiently.

"Sorry," Hen said. "Okay, where were we? K kept it…" There was a big circle in red ink around the text. In what Hen now recognized as Mrs. Nettles' handwriting was scrawled, *Yes, he did. But how? And where?*

Hen quickened her pace, anxiously scouring for more annotations. Now that she was looking, they were everywhere. Some in blue and some in red, little notes were strewn about the pages. She wanted to stop and scrutinize each scribble, but impatient Lilly wouldn't stand for it.

Once Hen had come to "X, Y, Z, and ampersand, all wished for a piece in hand," Lilly's eyes were shut and her head was heavy upon

Hen's chest. She closed the book and placed her sleeping daughter in her crib, anxious to examine the pages with the lights on in the living room. A quick kiss on the head, and Hen grabbed the book and snuck out to investigate. *Dang you, Mrs. Nettles. Why are you so compelling?*

Hen armed herself with two different colored pens and the only notebook she could find not filled with crayon scribbles. Sitting cross-legged with <u>A was an Apple Pie</u> open wide in front of her, Hen set to work. She turned the pages with a delicacy that she hadn't before. The book itself somehow seemed more fragile than it had a moment ago when she was just reading it aloud for a bedtime story. It had transformed into the courier of secret messages, like an old piece of parchment tossed in a bottle and then out to sea, waiting out the years to be washed ashore, found and read by its receiver. *Fascinating.*

She went through the poem more thoroughly this time, jotting down and organizing her thoughts, or rather Mrs. Nettles' thoughts, in her pink polka dot notebook. The annotations in red ink:

"K kept it"

Yes, he did. But how? And where?

"S stole it" was circled.

"T took it" was as well, but just the "T". In Mrs. Nettles' loopy handwriting:

I know what you've been doing, T.

Whoa, creepy, Hen thought to herself. She continued, this time recording the markings in blue:

"L longed for it" was circled. Beside it, an arrow pointing to "longed" was scrawled along with the words: *For me?*

"M mourned for it" had a question mark after it and written beneath:

Genuine? I surely hope my suspicions are wrong.

"V viewed it" was circled with another note:

We never had a viewing.

Hen also noticed a charcoal black pencil that circled "P peeped at it". *Debauchee,* it said. *Whatever that means,* Hen thought to herself.

This was crazy. It was basically a diary. A complicated, slightly creepy, and very cryptic diary. And Hen had not one, but twenty of them. *Crap.* So much for choosing to ignore it, this mystery was all too captivating. Hen sighed deeply and nodded to herself, *Okay, Mrs. Nettles, you win.* She was in.

CHAPTER FIVE

Hen's head hit the pillow with a heaviness that surprised even her. She was exhausted, every part of her; her eyes from scanning page after page for notations, her hand from furiously filling the polka dot journal (now fondly referred to as her *case file* because it made Hen feel like a real investigator) with notes and theories, her brain from attempting to unscramble a scrambled woman's ramblings, and her back from playing airplane with Lilly at the park for far longer than she originally intended.

Hen had delved deeply into three more of the books. The first was a book of nursery rhyme illustrations with no markings at all from Mrs. Nettles. The second book was the largest of the pile. Hen had been sure that it would be filled with annotations, but after relentlessly scouring through every page, she found only one: a phone number. It only had seven numbers, written prior to area codes, Hen assumed. She'd need to figure out the other three. Also, she needed to wait until morning to call anyway. No one is pleasant receiving a telephone call at 12:08 a.m.

The third book though, finally, contained a bit more of what Hen had been looking for. It was titled <u>An Anthology of Olde Rhymes</u>. One of the inclusions was a poem entitled "Lucy Locket".

Lucy Locket lost her pocket

Kitty Fisher found it

<u>Not a penny</u> was there in it

Only ribbon round it

Mrs. Nettles had underlined "not a penny". She also had written:

Sorry, Kitty. Go kill another old bird.

The creepiness of that line prompted Hen to take a break and come back to it later. So many books, so many rhymes. The task was daunting.

She had come across one familiar nursery rhyme earlier in the evening, "Lavender's Blue". There was no ink, no clues found upon its page, however, the familiar words brought back personal memories. It was a song she used to sing with Harry when they were first dating, one that they'd been surprised to realize they both sang as children. He'd refer to her as his queen and sing the little ditty *far too loudly* in front of anyone and everyone that would listen, gesturing and bowing to her. Though Hen would blush uncontrollably, she enjoyed the wholesomeness of it all. She liked the idea of being his queen. Hen had placed a sticky note in the page. Opening it once more, she read the first two lines:

Lavender's blue, dilly dilly, lavender's green

When I am king, dilly dilly, you shall be queen

With that, Hen smiled and closed her eyes feeling a little less lonely than usual.

Coffee. Breakfast. Snuggles. Ring around the Rosie with Lilly. *Now, that's a creepy nursery rhyme Mrs. Nettles would like.* Their morning routine was as it always was, which was not very routine-like at all. However, Lilly and Hen were both fed and dressed before 8:00 which was a success in Hen's book.

The wheels in Hen's mind were still turning as she wondered where to begin. There were so many unanswered questions and loose ends. She decided to start by figuring out the source of the phone number. It was the most straightforward clue, anyway. Hen knew that if anyone would be willing and able to help, it was Abby, so she typed a quick text.

"Hey girl. Random question, how do I go about figuring out the area code of an old number? I only have the last seven digits."

Hen opened her case file and typed in the phone number carefully to Abby. Send. She soon heard a sound on the front porch.

Clank... Thud. *Geez!* Hen thought to herself jumping an inch off the floor. The deliveryman had slammed the mailbox shut nearly breaking the lid and thrown a small package beneath it like he was chucking a football onto the ground.

"Does he hate his job or just me?" Hen wondered aloud. She opened the box. Nothing exciting. No slightly moldy envelopes. Hen wasn't sure if she was relieved or disappointed. Lilly had picked up the package and began carrying it around with her.

"Hey Lilly! Let's open that!"

"Bok," Lilly replied happily.

"Yeah! Let's open the box."

"No," Lilly said, looking up at her. One of her new favorite words.

"Why not?"

"Bok! Bok! Bok!" Lilly yelled and ran into the kitchen, package in hand.

"Lilly, please share!" Hen reminded, but Lilly had no intention of sharing. She walked around the house hugging the box close to her chest.

Please share. Hen found herself constantly saying those two words, mostly in situations like this where Lilly would then immediately run away with the item in question. Hen sighed then assured herself, *someday Lilly will learn to share.* She glanced over at her daughter, her tiny arms clutching the package for dear life. *Probably... eventually...* Lilly saw Hen looking over at her new prized procession and ran away with it to the living room. *This is toddlerhood,* Hen thought, rolling her eyes and smiling in spite of herself.

Hen waited impatiently and after about ten minutes, Lilly's interest had waned enough that she dropped the package, choosing to instead play with every single plastic container and lid that she could find. Hen cut through the tape and pulled up the cardboard flaps.

"Oh! Book!" she said, finally realizing what Lilly had been trying to say. "How did you know what was in here you smarty?" Lilly looked up from her plastic container avalanche, smiling proudly.

It was the library book. The one Hen had checked out for herself ages ago. Her business card was distinctly missing but in its place was a small paper card, just like the previous two. This one was without envelope and had an illustration on the front of a cheeky looking little boy, holding a pie, kissing a red-faced little girl in tears. *What a weird picture to put on a card,* Hen thought to herself.

As she opened the card, a twenty-dollar bill fell to the floor. Hen swiftly picked it up and read the card's interior message once again in loopy calligraphy. She noted the writing utensil this time, a smudgy black charcoal pencil was used for the body of the message, but just her name was written in black ink, like an after-thought.

Henrietta,

Have you ever heard it said that a picture tells a thousand words? What about film, could it be more? Out of crooked trees they fly as birds. Flocking to my fortune in herds. While he creeps in the shadows of what is in store.

This rhyme is terrible, Hen thought to herself. She flipped the card over.

This rhyme is quite terrible.

Hen laughed aloud. *At least she's honest.* She continued reading the backside of the card.

This rhyme is quite terrible. But heed its truths.
Act upon them and you will be able to do what I could not.
Mrs. Nettles

This message was far more puzzle-like than the others. It seemed to fit with the cryptic notes Hen had become so familiar with the previous evening within the pages of Mrs. Nettles' books. Thinking about this mystery as a puzzle to solve somehow made it far more approachable for Hen. It was more like a game and further removed from the reality of murder, or at least death.

She glanced down at her daughter, still knee-deep in lids and containers, fully immersed in whatever it was she was doing with them. Hen had a few minutes to think on Mrs. Nettles and her riddles.

She quickly wiped off the counter with a paper towel to be sure that it was dry then placed the card on the clean surface, open to its inscription along with the twenty-dollar bill. *Probably just to cover the library late fees,* Hen reasoned. She wouldn't spend it though, just in case it meant something more. Now to the card- *A picture is worth a thousand words. Pictures...like illustrations?* Hen snuck back to the spare room and grabbed the first book of three that she had scoured for clues last evening. It didn't have any handwritten notes, but it was full of illustrations.

She brought the book out to the kitchen so she could have an eye on Lilly. As she began flipping through its pages once more, she saw something oddly familiar. A picture of a goose wearing a bonnet, and not just any goose but one that she had seen before. She darted back once again to the spare room and returned to the kitchen with the other two cards. There she was. The same goose!

Hen looked back at the book. "Mother Goose" it said in tiny script on the lower left corner of the page. She glanced at the second card. Hen was fairly certain that she knew what nursery rhyme that one was from. Checking the table of contents, she promptly opened to an illustration of three fat little piggies matching the other. "The Three Little Pigs". *Of course. Mrs. Nettles had an odd obsession with nursery rhymes. She even bought the matching stationery set.*

The third picture was the trickiest. Hen hadn't the foggiest idea what it was from, so she had to painstakingly check every single page until finally, three quarters in, she found it. That cheeky little boy and that red faced girl. "Georgie Porgie" was written below.

Hen paused for a moment. Maybe she was on the wrong track. She didn't know what Georgie Porgie or any of these rhymes had to do with anything. Maybe Mrs. Nettles had meant a different type of picture entirely. *There were tons of portraits of her available to see online.* The cryptic message also mentioned video. *That opens a whole new can of worms.*

Hen sat down on the floor, frustrated. Uncomfortable, she sat up a bit and pulled a lid out from under her bum. Lilly giggled at her. Bing. Bing. Hen's phone went off as she received two text messages, back to back.

"So, you decided to investigate after all. I knew you would."

"Also, It's YOUR area code silly. That number is for an old antiques shop near you."

"Thanks Abby! But how did you know it had to do with Mrs. Nettles?"

"I called and talked to the owner for a second. Kind of grumpy old guy. He said his name was George Nettles-Brown. The Nettles name got me excited for you. You could be onto something!"

Hen stared at a different part of the shopkeeper's name. George. Georgie Porgie Nettles-Brown.

CHAPTER SIX

Hen pulled out of her mom's driveway, having just dropped off Lilly for the afternoon. The quietness inside the car that was at first soothing and relaxing was soon after empty and isolating. She wasn't one of those moms who couldn't wait to leave her kid. She missed her too much. As loud and crazy as Lilly could be, she was Hen's favorite companion.

She shook her head and switched the radio station in the car to a better song as if she were literally switching the station in her own brain. *Time to focus up.* Hen was on her way to The Great Golden Goose's Antiques. The coincidence of its name was certainly not lost on her.

Throughout the drive, Hen practiced what she would say, walking herself through several scenarios in her mind, so as to avoid a repeat of her interaction with the receptionist at the police station. The last thing she wanted to do was *give* information, she was there to get it. This reminded her of one of the poems she had read in the anthology.

A wise old owl lived in an oak,

The more he saw, the less he spoke

The less he spoke, the more he heard,

Now, wasn't he a wise old bird?

The GPS was showing she was close. It was a part of town Hen had never visited before. She may as well have been on the other side of the country. Parking her car in a lot, she pulled down the mirror to do a quick check before going in. Hen smiled at her reflection. She looked and felt pretty. Hen had actually taken the time to put on makeup and pick out an attractive, but not flashy outfit. She didn't want to stand out, but she certainly wanted to look presentable. Although as soon as she got home, those yoga pants were going right back on.

Deep breath. Okay, Hen, be confident and casual. Head held high, she locked the car and walked to the antiques shop. The giant golden block letters above the door were more reminiscent of a Chinese food restaurant rather than a retail store. They were worse for the wear with peeling paint and a bird's nest resting within the second "O" of "Goose's". The word "Antiques" was in small black lettering underneath as if it had been an afterthought. *Isn't that the most important part of the store's name?* Hen was always noticing things like that.

The door proved difficult to push open as if the wood had swelled twice its size in the humidity. In fact, Hen had so much trouble shoving it open, she nearly assumed that it was locked and the store was closed. She thought she'd give it one last vehement effort. Bursting through the door with a bang, she tripped in catching the eyes of two patrons and a saleswoman standing behind a long counter, all three of which were staring at her in silence. *So much for not standing out.*

Hen remembered her advice to herself from earlier, fought the urge to apologize for barging in, and instead decided to be confident and casual. She did, however, make a quick turn to the far corner of the store to avoid the stares from the three strangers.

Taking in her surroundings, Hen was increasingly glad that she didn't bring her one-and-a-half-year-old. *There are a thousand breakable things within Lilly's reach just in this corner of the room,* she thought.

She picked up a porcelain bowl shaped like a bunch of grapes with little eyes and mouths painted on each grape forming a disturbing bunch of tiny, creepy faces. Turning the bowl upside down, she noticed its price sticker. *$95 for that nightmare fuel.* She set it down gently and walked away slowly.

There were lovely, intricate items as well. A whole wall of antique brooches caught Hen's eye. One in particular struck her as uniquely beautiful. The pin was shaped like a dragonfly with caerulean gemstones on either side as its wings and tiny diamonds along the body. Two dazzling purple gems were placed at the ends of its curved antenna. It was huge and completely impractical for wearing in everyday life, but pretty to look at.

Hen heard the sticky door shut and realized she was alone in the store with the salesclerk. *Unless of course George Nettles-Brown is in the back,* Hen hoped. She walked to the front desk.

"Excuse me," Hen uttered.

"Yes miss, can I help you?" the salesgirl replied. Hen smiled inside at the notion of being called 'miss'. Perhaps she should take a little extra time to get ready more often. The salesgirl was pretty, young, and dressed to the nines, especially for working in a dingy old antiques store. Should Hen just ask her for George or try to play it cooler than that? She noticed that she was taking longer than usual to respond to the girl's question.

"I was wondering, um…" *Say something, Hen.* "I was wondering… about that dragonfly brooch. How much is it?"

"Amazing, isn't it? That's actually one of our specialty items. I would have to ask the owner about what he'd be willing to sell it for." *Perfect!*

"Oh okay, no problem. Could I speak with him?" *Effortlessly cool.*

"I'm sorry, ma'am. I'm afraid he isn't in today. Thursday is his usual day off. But I can make a note here to ask him for you." *Aw, shoot.*

"That's alright!" Hen blurted out. *Keep it cool.* "I mean, I can just come back in and speak with him about it later. That's no problem."

"If you insist. To be honest, he isn't the conversationalist."

"Oh really? How do you mean?"

"Well, Mr. Brown gets a little bit tiffed talking to customers. Talking to anyone, really. He hates talking to me. I actually don't know why he even hired me. I stink at counting money and I'm a bit of a klutz. I almost broke that terrifying grape bowl over there. I thought for sure it was going to haunt me." Hen smiled. She liked her, this girl reminded Hen a bit of a younger version of herself. "Sorry, I'm talking too much."

"No, not at all. I thought the same thing."

"Like a million creepy eyes peering into your soul," the salesgirl shuddered. "I'm Tammy by the way."

"Hen. It's Henrietta, but no one calls me Henrietta." *Except old Mrs. Nettles, of course.*

"Hi." Tammy's body language relaxed a bit. "So, what are you looking for?" Hen had learned that half-truths are always more believable than flat-out lies.

"Someone referenced this place to me recently and I was interested to learn more about it."

"Oh, well, we're just your standard antiques shop. All the items are curated by our owner, the Mr. Brown I was referring to earlier."

"Do people bring in items to sell?"

"No actually, it's only Mr. Brown's items here. I guess he has an eye for antiques. I don't know how he does it, but he finds the craziest stuff. People will pay a lot of money for the right type of antiques. He's having a bit of a dry spell I guess though because it's been a while since he has curated anything."

"Oh really?"

"Yeah. Maybe he just figured we have a big inventory of stuff, but usually that doesn't matter. Perhaps he just hasn't found anything worth selling lately. He's got an eye for what sells, like I said."

"Hmm, I wonder why that is."

"Well, he came from a prominent family at one point. He's actually a Nettles! His mom married into the family but remarried right after he was born. He got to keep the name though. I think he might be the last person left with the name."

"Oh, I thought you said his name was 'Brown'?" Hen was so proud of herself for being a wise old owl this time around, doing the listening instead of the talking.

"It's actually George Nettles-Brown. He likes to use his full name with customers and strangers on the phone and stuff, especially recently. He wants people to know he's a Nettles. Prestige and whatnot."

"Why recently?" Hen asked. Tammy leaned over the counter toward Hen and cupped her hand to her mouth like she was whispering to Hen the name of her crush at a sleepover party.

"The money," she murmured at last.

"Oh! I read an article about that." *That's true.*

"Yeah, he thinks he should be included in the will..." Tammy's words lingered in the air.

After a long wait, Hen finished, "But he's not?"

Tammy shrugged, "Dunno, but I'm pretty sure Essie Nettles hated him. Always called him 'Georgie'. He would go and visit her all the time and try to make it sound like she invited him, but I always got the feeling like she didn't. He hated her anyway. He'd leave me or Dana or Brooke or Leslie here alone all day and then yell at us immediately when he got back. He'd grumble to himself about being called 'Georgie' and how much he hated it. That's how I know."

"Gotcha." *Please keep oversharing, Tammy.*

"Yeah, I kind of loved how that old woman would tease him because, between you and me, he deserved it. Grumpy old man..." Tammy glanced down at her feet. "Sorry, I tend to talk too much."

"I don't mind at all." *True.* "I actually find it kind of interesting." *Now that's an understatement.* Hen gave her a genuine smile, which Tammy returned shyly. "Can I ask you a kind of personal question?" Hen inquired.

"Oh, uh, yeah, sure."

"Why *do* you work here? You seem to not be too keen on your boss. Or antiques. Or being a salesperson."

Tammy laughed, "I guess it's pretty obvious. I need the paycheck. I want to go back to school. I'm actually really interested in fashion, but I don't have the money to follow through on that, so I dunno.

Just trying to make ends meet right now, and Mr. Brown hired me. I didn't even apply. I just came in here with my aunt one day and he asked if I wanted a job. I jumped on the opportunity. It's been tough."

"Maybe he thought you looked like you knew what you were doing. Could have fooled me."

"It's amazing what a good outfit can do," Tammy said with a smile.

"You really do have an eye for fashion," Hen retorted.

"Thanks, but really, I wouldn't be this dressed up if it weren't in the dress code. It's pretty strict. I feel like half my salary goes to high end work clothes." Hen was surprised. *Why would an obsolete antique store have a strict dress code for its employees?*

The surprise must have been all over her face because Tammy responded, "Yeah, I know. I was surprised too. I always wear street clothes and change when I get here because I'm not trekking the whole way here in these heels and this skirt. The closest bus stop is still pretty far." Tammy's eyes moved toward an old cuckoo clock on the wall. "Oh my gosh! Is that really what time it is? I'm so sorry, I have like a million things to do and clean, but it was really nice talking with you, Hen."

"It really was." Hen truly meant it. She liked Tammy. She even felt a little bad for Tammy. She seemed lonely. Hen knew that feeling all too well. "Hey, do you maybe want to hangout sometime? You know, outside of an old antiques shop?"

"Where it always seems like someone is watching you including tiny creepy grape faces?" Hen and Tammy both laughed. "Yeah, that would be nice," Tammy said. The two exchanged numbers.

"Hey, could I use your bathroom?" Hen asked.

"I'm sorry, girl. It's employees only. Mr. Brown is a stickler about it."

"No worries," said Hen with a smile. With that, Tammy went back to work with the smallest feather duster Hen had ever seen. Hen was suddenly really thankful not to have this job. Tammy was basically dusting hundred-year-old dust off of a million tiny objects, wearing a skintight pencil skirt and red stilettos.

CHAPTER SEVEN

Hen decided to leave the store and go sit in a local coffee shop she had passed on her way. She looked around for Tammy to say goodbye before she left but couldn't find her, so she yanked on the old door and let herself out.

Once she'd finally used the restroom and was comfortably seated in a small booth in the coffeeshop, Hen pulled out her case file to jot down some notes of her conversation with Tammy before she forgot anything. She was trying her best to combat the fact that she really did have the worst memory.

The last thing Hen had written in her notebook was the "Georgie Porgie" poem.

> Georgie Porgie, pudding and pie,
>
> Kissed the girls and made them cry
>
> When the girls came out to play,
>
> Georgie Porgie ran away

Mrs. Nettles clearly thought old Georgie was up to something. Hen flipped back a few pages. The most recent note was copied into her own handwriting. Hen had noticed it was written in charcoal pencil inside the card with Georgie Porgie on the front. The pieces felt like they were frustratingly close to coming together.

Hen took a sip of her coffee. It was hot- a luxury that didn't go unnoticed. She opened up her phone to new contacts and stared at Tammy's name. She had just put her first name in Hen's phone when they had exchanged numbers. *What was Georgie up to? Did it have to do with Tammy?* Hen hoped not; she liked Tammy.

A light bulb went off in Hen's mind as she stared at the phone number below Tammy's name. *The phone number for the shop! It was written in charcoal, just like the message. They have to be linked. They both have to do with Georgie.* Hen was now calling Mr. Nettles-Brown 'Georgie' all the time. Now that she knew he hated it and seemed to be a jerk to Tammy, it was her own way of privately hassling him. On second thought, though, maybe she should not call him that to his face if she ever did get a chance to talk to him.

Something else was written in charcoal pencil. She couldn't remember what. *Shoot.* Hen sat racking her brain long enough to finish half her cup of coffee, then impatiently poured the remainder of her beverage into a to-go cup and hopped in the car.

She glanced at the digital clock on the dashboard. *Still too early to pick up Lilly.* She turned off the radio and put the windows down. She allowed herself a moment with her thoughts. *It was nice to talk to another adult person. What was it about that brooch that made it a specialty item? Georgie had known the late Mrs. Nettles personally. Why didn't Tammy think he had been welcomed when he went to visit her? There were so many old bits and bobs in the antiques shop, too many to fully take in.*

"I need to go back again," Hen reasoned to herself aloud, alone in her car.

Feeling empty-handed without a diaper bag and toddler on her hip, Hen marched inside her house and made her way directly to the spare room. She took a sip of the to-go coffee in her hand. *Aw man, cold.* Placing the cup on the desk, Hen reached the book she had been looking for, <u>A was an Apple Pie</u>.

There she saw it, in charcoal pencil, the word *'debauchee'* right beside 'P peeped at it'. A quick online search on her phone revealed its meaning.

Debauchee- one who gives in to sexual or sensual pleasures; a sexual deviant or pervert

Hen paused for a moment. It all made sense. Georgie Porgie kissed the girls and made them cry. He was a pervert, a 'peeper'. Hen suddenly remembered that all of the names of Tammy's fellow employees were women. Georgie had enforced a strict dress code that forced his female employees to wear stilettos and tight-fitting pencil skirts.

A chill went down Hen's back. She grabbed the Georgie Porgie card and read it once more.

Have you ever heard it said that a picture tells a thousand words? What about film, could it be more? Out of crooked trees they fly as birds. Flocking to my fortune in herds. While he creeps in the shadows of what is in store.

Hen took inventory of what she now knew. *Georgie wants the money, Tammy had said. He flocks to her fortune. Mrs. Nettles' missing fortune, of course. He's crooked? Some sort of crooked business deal?* Hen wondered. *Pictures, what pictures? The ones from the cards or something else? She mentions film. Something about a camera lens perhaps? Big brother watching...* Hen gasped.

She thought back to what Tammy had said about feeling like she was being watched.

"He creeps in the shadows of what is in store." *Of what is in store. In the store. The antiques store. He is watching his employees while they are in his store. It's why he hired Tammy on the spot. He liked the look of her and wanted to watch her, like her other female colleagues. Maybe ogling at them from behind a tiny pinhole like creepy guys in old movies. Maybe that's what she meant by 'film', a reference to an old film trope.* It was a sensible theory, anyway. Tammy had said that Georgie takes off on Thursdays. He was probably there, watching them the whole time. This thought nearly caused Hen to be physically sick. She was overwhelmed with an immediate responsibility for her new friend.

She drafted a text:

"Hey Tammy. This is Hen. Your boss is a pervert and he's watching you."

She paused and read it back. *Okay, coming on a little strong there.* Hen erased the text and typed another.

"Hey Tammy. This is Hen. Could you give me a call when you're done at work?"

Better. Besides, Hen didn't know for sure if he was watching her or what else he might be doing, but it certainly wasn't good. Georgie was up to something and gosh darn it, Hen was going to find out what.

CHAPTER EIGHT

With Lilly tucked soundly into bed, Hen hopped in the shower to wash off the ick of dusty antiques stores and debauchees. She suddenly felt very exposed. She thought of Tammy. Hen hoped that it wasn't too much, asking Tammy to call her. They didn't really even know each other. Awkwardness aside, Hen came to the conclusion that it was a good thing that she had reached out to her. *She needs to know,* Hen assured herself.

Just at that moment, her phone started ringing. Without hesitation, Hen jumped out of the shower, still dripping wet, and answered.

"Hello!" She exclaimed, lunging for the towel.

"Wow! Hi! That was such an excited hello." The voice on the other end was not Tammy. It was instead Harry.

Hen's voice lowered in volume a few levels, "Oh, yeah. Sorry." She gave a polite laugh. "I was just surprised. I was in the shower."

"Oh yeah?" She could almost hear him raise his eyebrows.

"Okay, okay." Hen laughed, but for real this time. "What's up?"

"Well, I just wanted to call you. To talk to you. Can I be honest?"

"Yeah, Harry, of course." He was speaking with in an uncharacteristically tender tone. Hen braced herself for the words 'just one more month'.

47

"I miss you."

A pause. Hen couldn't hold back the tears as they flooded down her already wet face.

"I miss you too," she said at last.

"This has been hard, me being away. I wish I could be with you and Lilly. And I know you've got everything covered but sometimes I worry about you..." His voice trailed off. Hen stopped for a moment. *Why would he be worried? What did he know?* She pondered a moment more until the wheels in her mind clicked: *his sister!*

"What did Jackie tell you?"

"Just that you were asking questions about an old woman who left behind a fortune. A fortune that is now missing."

"Yeah, I did ask her about that." *That was truthful.*

"Well, you don't need to. Hen, you actually don't need to worry about any of that. This new job is really promising. I know money's been a little tight over the past few years but that's why I'm here. I'm here to put myself in the position so we can finally be comfortable, so I can fully support my girls the way I want to."

Hen sighed in relief. Not at his words though. She really wasn't worried about their finances, at least not at the moment. She felt relieved at his lack of words. She had expected at least a mention about her involvement with the whole thing.

"That's really good to hear, Harry."

"So, you can stop fortune hunting," he chuckled. "I always promised you'd live like a queen, you know, and I intend to keep that promise." Hen gave a little smirk on the other side of the phone.

"You remember?" Hen replied, pleasantly surprised.

"Of course I remember. Lavender's blue dilly dilly…"

"Lavender's green," Hen finished.

Harry waited a moment then uttered just above a whisper, "Hey, Hen?"

"Yeah?"

"I've got to go but… I love you."

"I love you too, Harry." There was a bit of a pause.

"Okay, I'm glad." He hung up.

Hen put her damp towel on the hook and jumped back in the shower. After actually cleaning herself this time, she dried off again and changed into pajamas. Towel atop her head, Hen tiptoed to the kitchen to make a cup of tea. Now that she was finally showered and comfy with a peppermint tea in hand, she was ready to take on more of Mrs. Nettles' books.

The History of Rhyme seemed a promising title but contained no evidence that Hen could find upon first inspection.

My First Mother Goose Collection was her next pick, a children's book with durable pages for tiny hands. No pen marks, no charcoal pencil notes, however, tucked into the book toward the last few pages was a piece of folded paper.

It was a small, square sheet of personalized stationery, complete with an intricate ivy border and the name 'Nettles' hidden within the leaves in the upper left corner. To Hen's surprise, it wasn't a cryptic note but rather a drawing. She wasn't quite sure what it was supposed to be. It just kind of looked like a bunch of shapes. At the top of the page, (at least what she assumed was the top from the placement of the word 'Nettles'), was a skinny rectangle facing horizontally. Centered vertically on the left were two circles, one within the other, like a target. In line with the target shape were two other shapes. An oval on the middle-right and a tulip-looking shape with three bumps on the far left. So tiny, she almost missed it, there was a small 'x' drawn on this final shape.

Hen opened up her case file and did her best to recreate the drawing:

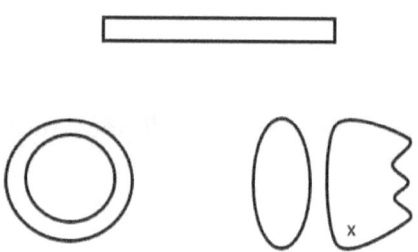

"What am I even looking at?" she whispered to herself aloud. She held her notebook in one hand, the stationery page in the other and examined them both. They looked the same. She did an excellent job of drawing… well, whatever it was. Hen was so deep in thought scrutinizing the two drawings that she nearly jumped out of her own skin when her phone started ringing again.

Heart pounding, she answered, "Um hi, hello?"

"Hey! Is this a bad time? Sorry its late. Oh my gosh, I just got done. Mr. Brown actually did come in today, which is really weird. He's never there on Thursdays. Anyway, had a million things for me to do, he's such a grumpy old curmudgeon…" Taking a breath and seeming to realize that she was talking too much, Tammy's voice resumed, "You said to call you?"

"No, not at all. I mean, no it's not a bad time and yes, I did say that. I'm glad you did."

"Oh good! What's up?"

"Well, you know how you said you felt like someone was watching you?"

Tammy laughed, "Yeah, I am so paranoid. I think it's just being around creepy old stuff all the time. I feel like that place might be haunted, you know?"

"Um, well…" Hen continued cautiously, "what if someone really was? Watching you, that is."

"You think it really IS haunted?!" Tammy retorted in disbelief. "I knew it! Wait, why?"

"Maybe someone a little less dead is watching you."

"You are kind of creeping me out," Tammy admitted.

"Sorry, I just have suspicions that Georg- I mean, Mr. Brown- is up to something."

"Oh! Ew, you mean you think Mr. Brown is watching me? I don't think so. His office isn't even close to the front desk. He's usually in there all day and days like today he only comes in toward the end of my shift… to yell at me," Tammy explained and then added, "He's such a jerk," under her breath.

"What if he was there though and you just didn't see him? Could there have been any way he was peeping at you when he said he was doing something else?"

"Hen, that's seriously creepy. I mean, I don't like him all that much, but I don't think so. There is nowhere he could be hiding other than his office, which, like I said, isn't anywhere close to the front desk. Even if he were peeping on me, he'd have to have binoculars with like serious zoom. What would he even be looking at anyway? Just watching me dust for hours?"

Hen paused and thought for a moment.

At last she asked Tammy, "What about video cameras?"

"We actually don't have any. It's too expensive to install them, I guess," she answered, then continued, "You really are serious about this, aren't you?"

"Yeah, I am. I know we just met, but I hope we can be friends. It really bothers me that someone might be taking advantage of you." *Maybe a little too honest, but sometimes the full truth is called for.* There was an uncomfortable pause and Hen worried that she'd come on too strong.

"That's…really nice. Thanks."

Hen smiled, relieved that she seemed to have won Tammy over.

"Okay," Tammy resumed, "so seriously, how do you know about Mr. Brown being 'up to something'?"

Hen hesitated. "Someone told me," she answered.

"Who?" Tammy wasn't accepting her half-truths at this point.

"Um, a former acquaintance of his."

"And that person's name is?"

Hen placed her palm to her forehead, conceding defeat. Begrudgingly she replied, "Mrs. Nettles."

"The dead Mrs. Nettles?" Tammy inquired.

There was an audible sigh from Hen through the phone. "Yeah." Hen waited for a moment for her new friend to reply.

Finally, Tammy shouted, "I knew it was haunted!"

Hen laughed out-loud. "Okay, not quite. But I guess it's only fair if I clue you in on what I know since you're already involved. Do you have a while?"

"All night!" Tammy said happily. "I love a good ghost story."

"Not a ghost story, but good…" And with that, Hen told Tammy the full (not ghost) story. She wasn't sure why exactly, but she trusted Tammy. Maybe she would come to regret it later, but it felt right in that moment, anyway.

Besides, Hen realized she had someone on the inside. Now, she was getting somewhere.

CHAPTER NINE

"So that's the plan. What do you think?" Hen asked her companion across the table.

"Gah!" Lilly replied happily. Hen had come to know that 'gah' was Lilly's way of saying 'good'.

"Yeah, I think so too," Hen said. Lilly wasn't quite the conversationalist yet, but she could still be a good listener. Hen liked to think that Lilly understood more than she realized. "How're your carrots?"

"Gah!" Lilly responded in exactly the same tone as before. *Is she just telling me what I want to hear?*

Hen glanced down at the polka dot notebook laid out before her. Tammy usually worked Mondays and Thursdays, however, she was off this Monday. That meant they would have to wait until that Thursday to have Tammy do any snooping. Hen would go back to the store one more time before then and inquire about the brooch and any other 'specialty' items. She would also be on the lookout for any false walls where someone could hide. Hen still felt certain that Georgie was there hiding when she was chatting with Tammy. In that case, he might recognize her. A chill went down her spine at the thought of him watching the two of them in secret. Perhaps she'd take precautions to dress differently and wear a hat in case that could help in some way.

Hen pushed her case file aside and pulled that morning's stack of mail toward her. *Dang.* Nothing interesting. She hadn't received any correspondence from Mrs. Nettles in days, just a lot of bills and credit card offers. *Big surprise there.*

Hen sat, twiddling her thumbs for a moment as Lilly finished most of the carrots on her plate and then threw the rest on the floor.

"Lilly, no, no," she scolded. Lilly's big beautiful eyes looked up at hers in remorse.

"We'd better clean them up, huh?" Hen replied in a softer tone. Lilly's smile was back.

"Keen up, keen up!" she sang.

After Lilly and Hen, but mostly Hen, cleaned up the floor carrots, the two spent the day running errands. Buying paper towels and mouthwash, getting the oil changed in the minivan- it all seemed so dull. Hen was in the middle of a real-life mystery, and yet the monotony and responsibility of everyday life persisted. *An odd phenomenon,* Hen thought to herself.

In the waiting room at the mechanic's shop, Hen made herself at home, moving a stack of magazines and emptying out a bag of blocks from the diaper bag onto the now bare coffee table. Lilly lit up with excitement and got straight to work building. She could get about five blocks high until she couldn't stand it anymore and had to knock them over. These particular blocks were one of the toys Hen saved exclusively for when they were on-the-go. Lilly could be entertained for upwards of twenty minutes with them, which is just about as long as you can do anything when you're one-and-a-half.

With Lilly occupied, Hen pulled out her phone and looked up info about old Georgie online. Having become accustomed to looking up information in Mrs. Nettles' books and letters, Hen almost forgot that she lived in the world of the internet. By no means was she a seasoned sleuth, however, a quick search turned up some interesting intel. Hen jotted it down in her ever-growing case file.

1. Georgie had no social media to speak of, not even a website for The Great Golden Goose's Antiques. *Every place of business has at least some online presence. Not very business savvy. Perhaps he didn't want to be found?*

2. There was a photo of him standing by the front door of his shop, though one wouldn't have known from the picture itself. Despite the golden letters having been cut off from the photo, Hen knew its location right away. *How perceptive!* Hen was proud of having recognized the entrance from her recent visit. Georgie was a balding man wearing an argyle sweater-vest. *He doesn't have to wear expensive shoes and tight-fitting clothes,* Hen observed, taking note of the double standard between him and his female employees. The photo did not look as if it were candid but somehow his expression made it seem as if he were caught off-guard by the photographer.

3. He had been interviewed following the death of Essie Nettles. He was 'unspeakably overwhelmed with grief' according to the article. He also mentioned not once but twice that he was the last remaining person with the Nettles name, although the author of the article clarified both times that he was not of direct lineage. Hen chuckled aloud at the thought of Georgie's blood boiling as he read that aside from the author.

4. He had been referenced once more following the mysterious disappearance of the Nettle's fortune. He had 'vehemently refused' to talk with the interviewer about his feelings on the matter. Instead he had complained about not receiving an iota from his birthright and had made his intentions of talking with his lawyer very clear.

Interesting, Hen thought to herself. She looked at the clock. Only five minutes had passed. Why did time drag so slowly at the mechanic's shop? Lilly was still happily building and knocking down towers. She continued her search by typing 'Essie Nettles' into the search bar and scrolling past the first few results, having read them already. Hen stumbled upon something interesting: a website detailing the history of still-standing Victorian Era mansions and the prominent families who lived there.

There it was, the Nettles Estate, in what must have been its glory days. It was gorgeous. The grandiose stone structure, complete with a tower fit for a fairy-tale princess, was dressed in ivy from top to bottom. The front gardens were filled with rose bushes in bloom.

Hen continued scrolling through more photos of the building itself. The more recent pictures displayed a dilapidated structure, in desperate need of care. *The Nettles Estate had declined in tandem with Mrs. Nettles herself.* Hen found herself saddened by this notion.

Finally, she stumbled upon pictures of the family, or rather, portraits. The family must have had a hundred pictures of themselves hanging within the walls of the Nettles Mansion. A number of the paintings were of Essie Nettles herself. Having been an actress, she was accustomed to having her likeness taken, or so the article said. Hen grinned a bit at the kookiness. *Was it Essie's idea to put her hand above her own head with the back of her hand on her opposite cheek looking surprised? That's a bold choice.*

Another portrait was her laying flat on her belly on a dining room table with an apple in her mouth. Hen laughed aloud at that one.

Then she came across a seemingly normal portrait in which Essie was painted alongside a man. *Perhaps her husband?* Hen took a closer look. Something about this particular painting was very familiar. It took her a minute, but then she saw it and knew for certain. The brooch! The exact dragonfly brooch from the antiques shop. There it was upon young Essie Nettles' tasseled shawl! *How did it come into Georgie's possession?*

Crash! Lilly had decided to add the stack of magazines to her tower and learned the important lesson of gravity as she attempted to climb it.

"Oh honey!" Hen jumped to her feet. "Are you okay?" Lilly, who was totally unharmed, noticed her mom's worried look and burst into tears. Hen scooped her up and rocked her for a moment as she calmed down. Then, she placed Lilly on the chair and started picking up the mess.

As she returned the first magazine to the rack, the cover caught her eye. Then, as she scanned one magazine after another, Hen began to notice a pattern. Every single cover was the same, a very large, white smile with the article title, "Giving Back- Derrick Tittle's Foundation of Inspiration". *After the fundraiser, they must have dumped all the remaining issues here,* Hen reasoned. She stacked them back up the best she could and threw away one magazine that was ripped badly. She didn't think anyone would mind as they had about twenty more copies of the same thing.

A tall, lanky man in light blue coveralls moseyed into the room and met eyes with Hen.

"Well, your van is basically beyond repair. We can scrap it for parts or try to fix it, but it'll cost 'ya about $15,000."

Hen stood there, stunned.

"What?" she finally blurted out in disbelief.

"Yeah, sorry about that. Plus, an extra $250 for the magazine." His eyes darted to the trash can then back to Hen. Then, he smiled a wide, white grin. *Oh, thank goodness he's kidding.* Hen's shoulders relaxed as she returned the smile. The mechanic chuckled and walked over to the register. His grease-stained coveralls were embroidered with the name 'Tom'. Hen watched him carefully as he punched numbers into the computer. Something was so familiar about Tom.

"Sorry for teasing 'ya," he said to break the silence. "Everything looks fine. Your oil's changed, and we rotated your tires for 'ya."

"Oh, okay good. Thanks, Tom," Hen replied.

"Tom?" He looked confused then glanced down at the embroidered letters. "Oh! Ha! Yeah, I am wearing Tom's old duds. I forgot mine this morning, so here we are."

"Oh." Hen felt her cheeks flush. Why did she feel embarrassed?

Not-Tom broke the silence again. "I'm Gene."

"Oh... hi. Uh, thanks... for the oil. And sorry, you know, about the magazine. Someone was being a little reckless." Hen gestured back to Lilly, still sitting like a perfect angel. *Of course! Now she chooses to sit quietly.*

"No worries. They're all old issues anyway. My cousin made me put out a million copies in the office 'ere so people would go to his shindig."

"Your cousin is Derrick Tittle." It was a statement, not a question. Hen knew why the smile had seemed so familiar. It was exactly the same smile that she'd just stacked up on the coffee table.

"Yep. He's alright, I guess," Not-Tom sighed.

"You guys don't get along?" Hen hoped she didn't seem too nosy.

"Nah, nothing like that. He's a character now. Like in a movie or somethin'. Like how an actor starts off playing a part, but that turns into him all the time. He *became* the part, ya know?"

"Everyone seems to love him," Hen said.

"Yeah, I guess he's lovable in that way. Does a lot for other people, so that's good on him." The conversation ended abruptly as Not-Tom turned around to grab the printed receipt from the machine behind him.

He placed the paper in front of Hen who signed it, then collected Lilly and the pack mule's worth of supplies needed for a day out running errands.

Staring down at her signature then back up at Hen, Not-Tom gave a little wave and a wink, "Thanks for stopping in, Miss Bellemore."

"Mrs." Hen corrected.

This time it was his turn to blush, "Oh, yes. Gotcha."

"Thank you. Have a nice day," she quickly responded and walked out.

Somehow the fact that Not-Tom was embarrassed made Hen feel a whole lot better about the awkwardness of their conversation.

Now that errands were complete, Hen was amped and ready to continue solving Mrs. Nettles' mystery. She glanced back at her sleepy daughter. *Well, after Lilly's nap anyway,* and then back on the case to continue solving this mystery!

CHAPTER TEN

It was the most studious Hen had felt since cramming for exams in college. Lilly, exhausted from playing architect at the mechanic's shop, fell straight to sleep the minute they got home, and graciously gave Hen the opportunity to fully immerse herself in the clues that filled the stack of books in her spare room. She scrawled pages of notes in her case file and taped within her notebook the various pieces of ivy-decorated Nettles stationery that had been tucked inconspicuously within the pages of several books.

Remembering once more that she lived in the age of technology, Hen pulled out her phone and snapped pictures of pages that seemed important so she could revisit them easily. She kept <u>A was an Apple Pie</u> and the book of illustrations together with her case file, sliding all three into an old school bag that she would toss in the car later.

Hen breathed a sigh of satisfaction, proud of herself for finally completing a once-over of all the books sent to her, a fairly daunting task to say the least. She went to the kitchen to grab a snack, maybe one of the hidden cookies since Lilly was still asleep, and, on her way, she caught a glimpse of herself in the hallway mirror.

Hair clipped back, reading glasses on, she would have thought she looked older, but somehow, she looked more like her younger self than she had in a long time. There was a vibrancy in her eyes, an energy that she hadn't felt in a while. The excitement of solving a mystery gave her that energy somehow. Perhaps she needed Mrs. Nettles just as much as she needed Hen. She thought about that for a second. *No, probably not. Mrs. Nettles was dead.* Hen had to keep reminding herself of that fact.

She began to formulate a list in her mind summarizing the wealth of cryptic clues that she had unearthed. *It was one of those skills you hone without even trying the minute you become a mom: list making.* For this particular list forming in her head, Hen noted that Mrs. Nettles' clues fit within one of five categories:

1. A suggestion that someone was stealing from Mrs. Nettles, or rather someone was stealing from someone else. (Hen assumed it had to do with the Nettles' fortune.)
2. An inference that someone Mrs. Nettles had once trusted had double-crossed her (and that she most certainly knew about it.)
3. A mention of lost love. *Sad, that one.*
4. A hint to, let's say, debauchery…
5. A clue that Hen found indecipherable for the time being, such as a cryptic picture or literary allusion she didn't understand or a loopy piece of handwriting that she couldn't quite make out.

A thief, a betrayer, and a pervert were all mentioned in Mrs. Nettles clues. Hen realized that Georgie Nettles-Brown could account for all three. It was about time she paid him a visit.

By the time sweet Lilly finally woke up, Hen was packed and ready to go. Without a babysitter available this time, Lilly was coming along for the ride. Hen decided to be optimistic and hope that she wouldn't break anything too expensive.

She didn't even need to plug the address for the antiques store into her GPS, she just remembered exactly how to get there, an odd phenomenon for Hen who got lost looking for allspice in the grocery store. It was as if being on high alert had heightened her ability to remember. Proud of her newfound directional skills, Hen whipped the minivan around, confidently pulling into the nearest parking spot. She pulled her hair into a low messy bun and threw on one of Harry's old ball caps. *Not so much a disguise as a bit of subterfuge.* Hen had heard that word in an old movie she'd seen once late at night in the early days of mom-hood when sleep wasn't much of a reality. *Subterfuge. Such a great word…*

Hen shook her head like she was erasing the picture on an old etch-a-sketch. Enough of her inner ramblings, it was time to confront Georgie face-to-face. She needed to focus. She wanted to talk with him, gain a sense of who he was and glean some information while remaining as inconspicuous as possible in the process. Hen tossed a single diaper in her purse and decided to leave the bulky diaper bag in the car. *One less reason to knock something over,* she reasoned.

She unhooked Lilly from her car-seat and made her way down the sidewalk until she found herself standing beneath the gold letters of The Great Golden Goose's Antiques. She remembered to yank the old wooden door exceptionally hard this time. It opened reluctantly with a creak. Big band music played softly from an old record player set up in the far corner of the store. Immediately, Lilly began to groove to the beat in Hen's arms. Hen smiled down at her and swayed a little herself, partly to the music and partly to keep her wiggly toddler from wriggling free.

A new scent tired to overcome the must. A strong scented candle had been lit with a potent cologne-like fragrance, but Hen still caught a whiff of mildew just the same. She made her way around the store, looking for anything out of the ordinary. She didn't have the 'eye for antiques' that Tammy referred to in their previous conversation and thus had no idea what she was even looking for. As her eyes darted around under the brim of her ball cap, she thought to herself, *it probably looks like I'm about to steal something.*

Suddenly, she locked eyes with someone else peering out from under a hat, his a striped fedora. Hen averted her eyes straightaway but for the half-second that the large, well-turned-out gentleman was within her vision, he struck her as familiar in some way. She felt his gaze linger upon her and quickened her pace toward the opposite corner of the store. *Didn't anyone teach him not to stare?* Hen pondered indignantly.

This thought reminded her of one of Mrs. Nettles' clues, "P peeped at it". More than anything else, that is what Hen was most interested in finding out. *Where was Georgie hiding?*

Hen set out to answer this exact question, but she didn't have to look far. Just before her, behind the register, was a balding man clad in the exact same argyle sweater she had seen him wear in the photograph online.

A pit formed in her stomach. All of a sudden, Hen was extremely nervous. She squeezed Lilly just a little tighter and started to make her way toward the counter and Georgie himself. On her way, however, the phone rang. Hen made a quick turn and found herself looking at a wall of old silk scarves. She gave the wall a little knock. Solid brick, not a false wall. She sighed, *cute scarves though.*

"The Great Golden Goose's, Mr. NETTLES-Brown speaking." Georgie's voice was whinier than Hen had imagined. She didn't miss his obvious emphasis of the 'Nettles' component of his name. "Oh, it's you. Well, most likely, yes, but it'll be upwards of $2000 plus, my…" his voice lowered to a whisper, "finder's fee." Hen kept pretending to not be eavesdropping and found herself holding a bright green scarf with ladybugs on it as she listened.

Georgie continued his phone conversation, "Well, that's what we agreed on. You know I have the best…" he paused for just a second as if ruminating on the correct word, "connections." After another short pause as the person on the other side of the phone spoke, Georgie chimed back in, "Okay then. It's yours. I'll set it aside for you… fine. I'll bring it to you. I can stop by today." There was another slight pause and then Hen saw Georgie glance up at her from out of the corner of her eye. "Look, we're going to have to talk about that some other time. I'll give you what you want, but you have to pay for it in full, that's all." He hung up the phone rather abruptly.

Hen suddenly realized that she was holding no less than six scarves. She laughed at herself and began hanging a few back up. Lilly seemed to be disappointed at the notion of putting all of the colorful scarves back.

"Tell you what Lilly Billy, let's each get one. One for you and one for me. Maybe we can even grab one for Grandma. What do you say?"

Lilly's face lit up. She scrambled to grab at the scarves on the wall, but luckily, Hen was standing far enough away that she couldn't reach.

"You can have *one*," Hen reminded Lilly. "Why don't you tell me which one you'd like, and Mommy will get it down for you."

"La-bug, la-bug, la-bug!" Lilly replied enthusiastically.

"Okay then! And how about I take…this one." Hen picked up a light pink shimmery scarf with scalloped edges. "And for Grandma, we can do…this one." Hen grabbed a light turquoise scarf with an intricate pattern of greens and blues mixed in.

Hen took a deep breath. It was time. The plan was to make small talk while she checked out, getting him to open up as she had with Tammy. It was a bit more nerve-wracking to talk face-to-face with the man she had been investigating, the man that Mrs. Nettles knew was up to something. What exactly was he up to? Would he recognize her? She swallowed the lump in her throat and decided to go find out.

Placing the scarves on the table, she cleared her throat to get his attention and said politely, "Excuse me, I'd like to purchase these scarves."

Georgie turned around and immediately glowered at Hen, his eyes traveling up and down scrutinizing her. If he recognized her at all, he was very careful not to show it. Hen also noticed that he seemed highly unenthused with his first impression of her because he immediately looked back down at the counter with a grimace and picked up each scarf with pudgy fingers, carefully examining each tag.

Eyes still fixed on the counter, he grumbled, "The green one is five... The pink one is five... and the turquoise one is seven fifty."

"That's fine," Hen replied as she reached for her wallet. "If you don't mind me asking, why is that one two dollars and fifty cents more?"

"No." Georgie glared at her down his nose as if he were royalty and Hen was the servant who spit-shined his shoes. "Seven fifty. As in seven hundred and fifty dollars."

"Ha!" Hen responded, then saw instantly that he wasn't kidding. "Wait, $750 for a scarf?"

"It's a *specialty item.*" He said the last two words slowly and condescendingly, as if he were talking to a small child.

Hen stopped herself from scoffing. "What makes it special?" she asked calmly. Georgie let out an audible sigh of annoyance.

"It's rarity," he said back as if this conversation were boring him beyond belief.

"Do you have a lot of specialty items here?" Hen inquired.

"Are you going to buy the scarf or not?" he blurted.

Hen was caught off-guard by the bluntness and utter rudeness of his reply.

66

"Um, yes. I mean, I'll take these two. You can keep that one." She pushed the turquoise scarf back toward him and put cash on the counter. If she hadn't promised Lilly a scarf, she definitely wouldn't have supported this guy's business. *What a jerk.*

Having been so distracted by her conversation with Georgie, Hen had hardly noticed Lilly in her arms leaning further and further toward the lit candle that sat on the counter between them. Before she had time to pull it away, Lilly's tiny fingers reached toward the hot wax. Though Hen quickly snatched it away from the flame, it was too late. Little Lilly touched the melted wax and burst out into tears. Hen felt absolutely awful.

"Where is your restroom?" Hen frantically asked Georgie.

"It's for employees onl-"

"WHERE IS IT? I need to run her hand under cold water. NOW!" Hen found herself screaming.

Georgie suddenly lost the smug look that had been plastered on his face and pointed dejectedly toward the back corner of the store.

"Thank you." Hen marched toward the bathroom kissing poor Lilly and her tiny hand the whole way.

"You'd better be quick, I have to leave in a minute!" he called after her.

Hen ignored him and rushed through the bathroom door, turning on the faucet. She placed Lilly's burned hand under the water and rubbed it gently to get off the tiny bit of wax that remained.

"Aw, baby-girl. I'm so sorry that Mommy let that happen." Lilly's crying subsided and quieted to sniffles. After a minute or two of holding her hand under the water, she had stopped crying completely. "How does your hand feel now, baby?"

"Cold," Lilly replied.

Hen laughed. "Well, that's good. Let's just hold it here for a second more, okay?"

Hen looked around the restroom. It was very sparsely decorated, especially compared to the cluttered store's interior. The door was to her left, a toilet behind her, pedestal sink in front of her and an antique looking mirror on the wall above the sink. Lilly started to squirm a bit.

"I have to go!" Georgie grumbled from outside the door.

"Fine," Hen replied. If she didn't hate this guy already, she definitely did now. She dried Lilly's hand and looked at the mirror. The shape of it, with three bumps at the top, was so familiar. Lilly continued to squirm in her arms, catching her foot on the bottom corner of the mirror. As she did, it swung back and forth, like it was on a pendulum, instead of mounted with wire. This piqued Hen's curiosity, so she pushed the mirror to the side. As it swung slightly to the left, she noticed something out of the ordinary. Hen could swear that she saw a miniscule but deep compartment laying behind the mirror. *What is that insufferable Georgie hiding back there?*

Bang! Bang! He was pounding down the door.

"I have to leave!" he screamed from the outside the bathroom. The exploration would have to wait. She gave Lilly an extra squeeze and opened the door.

Hen looked Georgie straight in the eyes and said, "I'm leaving." She rushed past him, grabbed her scarves off the front counter and walked out.

Lilly was back to her smiley self, thank goodness, and her hand seemed to be fine after all. The whole walk to the car, Hen replayed the unpleasant interaction with Georgie. *Who had he been talking with on the phone? Was that why he was in such a rush to leave? Why was that scarf so absurdly expensive? Could it have once belonged to Mrs. Nettles just like the dragonfly pin? And most importantly, what was behind that mirror?*

CHAPTER ELEVEN

With everyone safely strapped in, Hen drove off to the peaceful park she and Lilly had discovered recently. *When was that exactly? Yesterday? Last week?* The days were certainly starting to blend together.

Luckily, she had saved the park's address in her phone so she could find her way back. Her hands were shaking with anger and frustration. How could she have let Lilly stick her hand in hot wax? She felt like a terrible mom. And how big of a jerk was Georgie in person? He almost didn't let her run Lilly's hand under cold water after *watching* her burn herself. Did he not want them to go in the bathroom because he was afraid of what she might find? Why hadn't she just taken one extra minute to find out what was behind that mirror?

Hen grunted aloud in frustration. She felt like just about the worst detective and the worst mom in the world. Hen decided to do what she often did when she was feeling down and began to dial Abby.

"Hello, Henny!" her friend cheerfully answered.

"Hey," Hen replied, her tense shoulders relaxing a bit at the comfort of a familiar voice on the other end.

"What's wrong?" Abby always knew when something was wrong, sometimes before Hen did herself.

"Well, I just met George Nettles-Brown."

"Was he just as much of a grump on the phone with you as he was with me?" Abby asked.

"Yeah, you could say that, except it wasn't on the phone..." Hen continued to tell Abby of her experience in the antiques store, careful not to leave out any details. It was almost as good as writing them down. After Hen finished, Abby paused for a moment.

In an uncharacteristically serious tone she replied, "Oh my gosh, Hen. I can't believe you went to see him in person. And that you brought Lilly! You've got to be more careful."

It wasn't the response Hen had expected. The remark about Lilly stung the most, hitting a nerve as she already felt mom guilt prior to the phone call.

"Well, I didn't mean for her to get hurt," she answered, finding herself strangely defensive.

"No of course not! I'm sure she'll be okay. I mean, the fact that you both were face-to-face with this guy..."

"What do you mean?" Hen inquired, irritation in her voice.

"Henny, what mystery do you think you're solving?"

Hen didn't know how to answer that question.

An awkward bit of silence was broken by Abby finally blurting out, "He could be Mrs. Nettles' murderer! That's where the clues were leading you, right?"

Hen once again didn't immediately respond. She hadn't even considered that Georgie was, in fact, a murderer.

"You think he... *murdered* Mrs. Nettles?" she asked Abby, almost in a whisper.

"I don't know, but maybe. What was the first thing Mrs. Nettles asked you to do? Don't you remember?"

"Figure out...who killed her." Hen paused, "But... but she died of old age. She was a kooky old lady."

"Maybe," Abby replied softly. "Although, she had suspicions of this George guy. You probably should too."

Hen realized that her minivan had been idling in a parking spot for far too long at this point.

"Hey," she couldn't disguise the aloof tone of her voice, "we're here, so I'll talk to you later."

"Aw, Hen, don't be mad. I'm just worried about you guys."

"Not mad. And don't worry about us. I've got this. I have to go though."

"Okay, but call me later, will you?"

"Yep. Bye."

"Bye."

Hen could hear Abby's dejection in that last 'bye', but she decided not to concern herself with that for the time being. She was a little angry that Abby had been so patronizing, and also a little angry at herself for not having considered the possibility that Georgie was a dangerous man. She had brought her beautiful little daughter into that situation. What kind of mother was she?

Hen slumped onto a bench and felt her eyes begin to well up with tears. Lilly, who was playing in the mulch, seemed to know exactly what Hen needed in that moment. She toddled toward her and laid her little head gently on Hen's lap. All the tears that had already formed immediately started falling down Hen's cheeks, but by the time they had rolled down her face, they had transformed from tears of anger and frustration to those of grateful relief.

Hen was suddenly overwhelmed by just how glad she was that Lilly was okay. As much as she hated to admit it, Abby was right about pretty much everything. If she was going to continue solving this mystery, she needed to be more careful. Hen made a vow to herself right then and there that she would not put herself or especially Lilly, in a dangerous situation.

Lilly grabbed onto Hen's hand and tugged for her to come. Hen obliged, following her daughter through the park and around a large hedge. Hen was once again blown away by the beauty of the park. A huge walk-through public garden was bursting with color before them. Lilly and Hen made their way down a stone path and stopped to admire blossoming flowers and spirited wildlife. They must have spent at least twenty minutes watching a family of robins skittering through a field. The mother and daughter pretended to be robins themselves, hopping and chirping and digging for worms in the dirt. Hen thought back to one of the rhymes from Mrs. Nettles books that went something like:

Little Robin Redbreast sat upon a rail

Niddle, nobble went his head,

Widdle, waggle went his tail.

Little Robin Redbreast came to visit me

This is what he whistled:

Thank you for my tea.

Hen smiled at the idea of having tea with the birds hopping about in the public garden. She thought of Mrs. Nettles, wearing her turquoise scarf and dragonfly pin, finding joy in that same poem. If only she were still alive, Mrs. Nettles could answer some of her burning questions.

Hen pondered for a moment when a thought came to her. *Someone* was sending her mail. Someone alive. A dead person can't go to the post-office by themselves. Whoever it was that sent her those letters had to know more. Hen leapt up and ran back to the car through the garden with a giggling Lilly. It was time to do some more digging. But this time, not for worms.

CHAPTER TWELVE

Lilly and Hen settled back in the car, and Hen put on a CD of kiddie songs to keep her little one entertained. She sat in the backseat with the windows down in her parked car, scrolling through her phone for a clue as to who could be sending her Mrs. Nettles' messages while periodically giving Lilly snacks.

It was more difficult than she imagined, finding people connected with Mrs. Nettles. So many of the articles were about the woman herself, her work on the stage, her crazy antics. She was almost always photographed or painted alone, or amongst a crowd of blurred faces. However, Hen did stumble across an old black and white photograph of her with a short man with a mustache. The photo was captioned "Essie Nettles with husband, Francis, on holiday". Francis didn't even get a last name in the text. He appeared to be an unassuming man, so perhaps he didn't mind this excluded detail. Hen looked closely at the photo. *They seemed happy, Essie and Francis.* Hen wondered when the last time a picture had even been taken of her and Harry together. And if they did find a recent snapshot of the two of them, would Hen and Harry have looked as happy as the black and white faces before her?

It couldn't have been Francis that had contacted Hen, however, because as she read on, she was reminded that he preceded his wife in death by over a decade. Interestingly enough, he had been proclaimed dead after having gone missing for several months. The article didn't say much about the man besides that he enjoyed tinkering in his workshop and wore brightly colored vests to every occasion. Mostly, the article only described Francis by his role that he seemed happy enough to play, that of the man behind the great woman.

Hen sighed in frustration. *Who else then?* Hen pulled out her case file and began to scribble some dates and details of the unforgettable Essie Nettles. As a topic of gossip columnists, Hen wasn't sure what was fact or fabrication, but she wrote down all of her acquisitions about Essie anyway. Mrs. Nettles had no children of her own but did work with charities to help underprivileged youth. *That's awesome,* Hen thought to herself. She handed Lilly a snack and continued browsing the article, "An avid reader with a love of puzzles and nursery rhymes even into adulthood."

"That's an understatement," Hen said to herself as she read. Mrs. Nettles and Essie Nettles seemed like two different people to her before this moment, almost as if they were separate characters: one, a lively, beautiful starlet, and the other, a paranoid and lonely, eccentric old woman. Yet, as Hen compiled more details about a long life lived, Mrs. Essie Nettles seemed more real and interestingly complex than before. As she considered an elderly Mrs. Nettles, living alone in that old decaying mansion, it was a bit heartbreaking. Maybe she should pay that old mansion a visit.

After a brief search, Hen came to learn that the Nettles Mansion was a mere forty-five minutes from her current location, tucked away in the forest past some winding roads, according to the GPS on her phone. It didn't seem like the most visitor-friendly place as they didn't have tours or anything. *Bummer.* The article didn't specify who would take over the mansion now, only that it sat uninhabited since the death of Mrs. Nettles and warned against trespassers entering the old building.

Lilly looked up at Hen, hand outstretched. Hen reached into her lap for another snack to hand her daughter and realized that she only had one more. *Time to go, I guess,* Hen thought to herself. She gave Lilly the last snack and jumped into the front seat to head home.

Halfway there, a tuckered-out Lilly dozed off. Hen glanced at the clock on the dashboard: second naptime. She'd been down this road before, if she woke up Lilly to bring her inside, she would never fall back asleep, which meant she would be all out of sorts when it came time for bed. Hen was stuck driving around for a while.

She pondered for a moment where to go before realizing that she had an address already plugged into her GPS for the Nettles Mansion. *No time like the present!* Hen changed the music… anything was better than Lilly's kiddie songs that she had heard a million times. A classical music station was the first thing that she found, poking around blindly as she kept her eyes on the unfamiliar road. It was soothing and soft, the perfect vibe for an elongated drive with the company of a sleeping toddler. *That will do.*

The longer she drove, the deeper into the woods she found herself. Though it was still light out, the sun nearly disappeared under the dense trees. The skinny, winding road became harder and harder to see. It was more of a hiking path than a road at all. Hen took her time but felt herself becoming anxious as she drove through unfamiliar territory. A feeling washed over her as if she shouldn't be there.

There is nothing wrong with going to see the mansion from the outside, Hen assured herself. She was pretty sure that what she was doing wouldn't be considered trespassing. She only wanted to take a quick look and get a feel for the place.

Luckily, there was only one road and one way to go because Hen found herself in and out of service, unable to use the GPS in various parts of the drive. She started to second-guess herself all the same, wondering if she was, in fact, going the right way or just driving aimlessly through the forest. At that moment, the trees, and the shadows they produced, began to clear, revealing a long driveway lined in overgrown rose bushes leading to what Hen could only assume was her destination.

The Nettles Mansion was beautiful. Huge and slightly ominous, but beautifully ornate, though nature had begun to reclaim the architecture from the outside. Ivy covered almost every wall. Hen slowed down at first to admire the building, but suddenly came to a dead stop in the driveway. She paused a moment. Something felt wrong. Perhaps this *was* trespassing.

A lump formed in Hen's throat. She had her sweet baby in the backseat, and she had promised not to put them in any situation that could lead to danger. The classical music station was now playing something brooding in a minor key, providing the foreboding soundtrack to Hen's already uneasy mind. She gave another look at the mansion. It looked lonely, cold. As she quickly scanned the building to take it all in, something caught her eye. She swore she saw a flash of red in the upstairs window, like a curtain swooshing closed.

Her heart beat loudly in her chest, this old place was supposed to be abandoned. Did someone know she was here? Before she could think any more on it, a deer jumped out from behind the thick hedges, nearly bumping into her car and making her jump herself. Hen gave a squeal and immediately put her car in reverse to back out of the driveway. Lilly drowsily opened her eyes and began crying after that startling awakening. The music crescendoed while Hen peeled out.

Once safely back on the winding road home, Hen swapped out the ominous music for Twinkle, Twinkle Little Star and took a deep breath, hands still shaking and heart still pounding. After a few pouts and sniffles, Lilly rested her head and looked out the window quietly.

Hen's mind started to cycle through a list of questions. Why had she felt so uneasy as she approached that old mansion? What was it about the place that made her feel that way? Was that just a trick of the light or was there really someone there watching her from the window? Could that be her mystery mailer?

After making it back to her own driveway, Hen was overwhelmed by gratitude. She had no desire to live in a place like the mansion she just saw. Her house was small and messy, but it was warm and cozy and full of Lilly giggles. As she carried Lilly on her hip into the house, Hen felt her phone buzz in her pocket. It was Tammy.

"Hey girl. I got called in tomorrow. I guess Brooke is sick. Anyway, I'm ready to be a spy if you still want me to. What do I need to do?"

CHAPTER THIRTEEN

Hen took her time to develop a plan for her friend. She wanted to keep her promise to prevent anyone from being in harm's way and to make it as safe as possible for Tammy. If Georgie left the building at any time, Tammy could inspect behind the mirror. She would video her findings to send to Hen. Also, if she got the chance, Tammy could sneak into Georgie's office to look for anything suspicious, snapping photos for Hen.

Hen stressed for Tammy to not take anything and to leave not a trace so that Georgie wouldn't suspect anything after she left.

"Got it!" Tammy had texted back.

Then Hen played the waiting game. She struggled to sleep that night on pins and needles in anticipation. The next morning, she woke up extraordinary early, fixing herself an omelet and some coffee. The minutes and hours passed slowly.

Once Lilly woke up, Hen was appreciative for the distraction, but nonetheless, she couldn't get her mind off of Tammy at the antiques store. What was she going to find behind that mirror? Was Georgie in fact dangerous like Abby had suggested? Hen hoped that Tammy would be smart and keep safe.

Other than Hen's distracted thoughts and checking of the clock nearly every twenty minutes, the goings on of the day were strangely and pleasantly normal. Given the rainy day outside, Hen pulled out the art supplies for Lilly, and the two girls colored, painted, and decorated with stickers. They cuddled and watched a movie as well. Later, when the sun finally poked its head through the thick clouds, they ran outside to splash in puddles together.

Hen felt guilty for being so distracted from what was actually a really fun mother-daughter day with Lilly. She felt guilty for having sent someone else to do the dirty work at the antiques store, though she knew it needed to be Tammy regardless. She felt guilty for having eaten an omelet that morning and giving Lilly dry cereal once she woke up because she didn't feel like dirtying another pan. *Guess that's just something else that comes with motherhood, list-making and guilt,* Hen thought to herself.

Finally, after what seemed like an eternity, Hen's phone rang in the late afternoon.

"Hello?" she answered in anticipation.

"Hey! Mr. Brown is out, and I am snooping around like a regular detective," Tammy responded excitedly.

"That's awesome! Did you find anything?"

"Well not yet. He just left. Where exactly am I looking?"

"I'd start behind the mirror in the bathroom."

"Like where exactly?" Tammy inquired.

"If you push the mirror over, you'll see a little compartment. At least I think that's what I saw," Hen explained.

"Um… Hmm…Okay." By her hesitation, it was obvious to Hen that Tammy was not looking in the right place. Tammy sighed, "I wish you could just show me real quick."

Hen thought for a moment, "Hold on, I'll draw you a little map, so you know what I'm talking about." Hen grabbed a crayon and a piece of yellow construction paper with monkey stickers slapped all over it off the floor. Flipping over the paper, she drew a little map of the bathroom with a small 'x' marking the location of the hidden compartment. She snapped a picture and texted it to Tammy.

"Oh okay, gotcha!" Tammy responded once she'd received Hen's map. "So, I just…push this over…somehow…oh wait!"

"What?"

"Yuck. I have to stick my fingers in this hole in the wall?"

"I mean, yeah, probably." Hen wished she was there. She would have already discovered what was hidden back there by now.

"It's a little…electronic thing? Hold on, I think this is a camera. There's a little lens on it. Oh my gosh! I think it's recording right now! There's a little blinky light thing."

"A camera?" Hen asked. *The "video" Mrs. Nettles had mentioned. How could she have known about a hidden camera in the bathroom of the antiques store?*

"Yeah. What the heck is it even recording? People using the bathroom?" A pause. "Oh my gosh, Hen, I have been naked in this bathroom like hundreds of times. Do you think Mr. Brown has been recording me? Is that why I need to change before I start my shift?"

"Well…maybe, but maybe he didn't know about it," Hen offered to soften the blow, though she knew in her gut that wasn't true.

"You know what? Screw him. This place is empty. I'm going to check his office right now." Tammy spoke with a tone that Hen hadn't heard from her before. Hen didn't know her all that well, but she could tell that Tammy was livid.

"That dick!" Tammy yelled, obviously having discovered something else. "That little perv!"

"What?" Hen couldn't help but ask.

"He has his computer open and it's literally a video feed of this camera!" Tammy said in disgust. "I cannot believe this! No security cameras, so it's okay if the place gets robbed while I'm working the counter but he has a live feed of the bathroom so he can watch me get undressed every time I come in and leave from a shift?"

"I'm so sorry, Tammy. That's gross."

"Yeah. It is," she replied. Hen heard a bunch of clattering about from the other side of the line.

"What are you doing now?" Hen asked.

"I'm going to call you back in a bit, okay?" Tammy replied.

"Wait, did you take a video, so we have evidence?"

"Oh yeah! Let me hang up and get the evidence."

"Okay, but be careful, alright?"

"Mmhmm. Call you back in a minute." Tammy abruptly hung up.

Whoa, ew, so Georgie was watching from a peephole, but it was a peephole with a camera inside. Mrs. Nettles was right. He was a debauchee.

Hen began to clean up the house as a means of distraction while she awaited Tammy's call back. She grabbed the yellow construction paper that she had used to draw her makeshift map. Her drawing looked so similar to one she had seen before, but where? *Mrs. Nettles first drawing on the ivy-lined paper!* Hen looked up her recreation of the drawing in her case file and ascertained that they were one in the same.

The drawing pointed out exactly where to find the hidden camera. It was a map with 'x' marking the spot! How did she not see it before? Hen flipped through the notebook to where she had taped in two more drawings. Both had x's in them. She had two more unmarked maps. *Leading where?* she wondered. Before Hen had much time to consider this new discovery, Lilly grabbed the yellow paper from her hand and flipped it over.

"Monkeys!" she squealed, pointing out the stickers. Hen scooped her up and gave her an extra tight squeeze. She wanted to protect Lilly from all the Georgie's of the world. At least she could keep her from this one.

Hen only wished she could have protected Tammy as well. This thought caused Hen to realize something, and she picked up the phone to dial her new friend back.

"Hey! I was just going to call you!"

"Hey Tammy, I just realized, if that camera was recording you, maybe you should take it so that Geo- I mean, Mr. Brown, doesn't know that you are the one that found it."

"Way ahead of you!" she responded gleefully. Tammy's tone was no longer angry, in fact, she sounded downright giddy.

"That's good thinking," said Hen, sighing in relief.

"Yeah, I took videos of everything…and then I just starting taking everything. You know, just to be safe."

"Everything?"

"Yeah, the camera from behind the mirror, and also some logbooks, a few of the *specialty* items, his computer…"

"Wait, Tammy, that's definitely stealing."

"Well, I don't really care," Tammy replied indignantly. "Besides, I'm only taking that which has already been stolen." Hen paused for a minute.

"What do you mean?" she asked.

"Not only has that scumbag been watching us from his creepy camera in the wall, but I think he's also been selling stolen goods. I got a look at some of his files. Which means, I have been selling stolen goods, without knowing it. Some old lady's stuff, snatched right out from under her nose…family heirlooms that should be passed down to children or grandchildren, and here we've been profiting off of them. I feel awful about that. So, I'm going to put things right."

"That's very noble of you. But I don't want you to get in trouble."

"Yeah, I thought maybe you'd have an idea about what to do about that…" Tammy's voice trailed off. Hen sighed. She was really coming to like Tammy, but she could be just a little bit of an airhead.

"Okay, look. Meet me in fifteen minutes. We'll just drop it off at the police station and they can do with it what they will."

"Great!" Tammy hesitated for a moment, "Sorry I got carried away."

"It's okay," Hen smiled.

"Guess I'm out of a job now, huh?"

Hen felt a pang of guilt, "Oh, I don't know. One thing at a time, hey?"

"It's okay," Tammy replied. "This was worth it."

CHAPTER FOURTEEN

Hen found an old, unused moving box collecting dust in her closet which she brought along with some packing tape and a permanent marker. The new plan was to dump Tammy's evidence in the box and leave it for the police to go through. Neither Tammy nor Hen were seasoned detectives, so the evidence collected would be much more useful in the hands of the police. Hen and Lilly were back in the car and on their way to see Tammy.

Once the two women met up and Tammy had the chance to gush over how cute Lilly was, they organized the hoard of stuff in the back of Tammy's car, *sort of*, and Hen drove it straight to the police station. Though Tammy wanted to come with her, they decided that it was probably better if Hen went alone. Hen was up for the task keeping to herself the uneasy feeling she was experiencing. She wasn't exactly comfortable driving around with a box full of stolen items in her car and was anxious to get rid of them as soon as possible.

Luckily, Hen had no trouble finding a parking spot this time around. However, she did have a bit of trouble actually making her way into the building. The last time she found herself at the station, she had been completely ill-prepared and embarrassed, but this time, she had the potential to actually get in serious trouble. Hen wasn't quite sure how to get the box of evidence to the police but also separate herself from the incriminating items inside.

She pulled out her case file and yanked a piece of blank paper from the back of the notebook, jotting down a memo to the police that explained the box's contents, leaving out a few choice details: Hen's and Tammy's names and any mention of Mrs. Nettles' clues that led Hen to The Great Golden Goose's in the first place. She was sure to mention the brooch and scarf and her suspicions that they were, in fact, stolen from their original owner.

Hen held the flimsy paper in front of her, inspecting it quickly before folding it twice and laying it in the box in plain sight. *Okay, make this quick and painless*, she thought to herself. As she hopped out of the car to grab the box from her trunk, a voice greeted her from behind.

"Fancy meeting you here, Mrs. Bellemore," Hen's nerves got the better of her and she nearly jumped out of her skin, turning around so hastily that she banged her elbow against the corner of her open trunk.

"Ouch!" she called out, grabbing her injured elbow. Hen looked up to see Thad. Why was he always hanging around the police station? "Oh, hey," she responded half-heartedly.

"Sorry, didn't mean to scare you." He was looking at her with apprehension now. It was no wonder, she probably looked extremely suspicious.

"Oh, yeah… No, it's fine," Hen blurted out.

"So, you moving in?" Thad asked, graciously ignoring Hen's awkwardness.

She gave a polite laugh. "Oh this? No, I just have some stuff to drop off."

"Donations? You probably want the community center building."

"Well, not exactly."

Thad thankfully did not pry any further. "Okay. You need help? It looks kind of heavy."

Hen thought for a moment. That was perfect! Thad could just drop the box off at the policeman's desk and she didn't have to be involved at all.

"Actually, yeah, that'd be great," Hen replied with a smile.

She told him where to put the box and, despite the risk of sounding even more suspicious, kindly asked that he just drop it off without looking inside. There was no reason for Thad to get involved. The less he knew, the better. He was all too accommodating. After a quick goodbye, he headed inside, box in hand.

Hen closed her trunk and returned to her perch behind the wheel, watching Thad lug the box into the building. Hen got a bit nervous when he stopped briefly to talk on the phone, placing what Hen knew to be evidence of Georgie's guilt carelessly on the ground for a moment. But shortly after, he picked it back up and headed in. He seemed to be sticking to his word because she didn't see him look into the box even once. *Thad actually turned out to be a pretty okay guy as an adult*, she thought to herself. What's more, Hen didn't have to be involved any further and for that, she was truly grateful. *So, that's case closed… right?* Something told her that it wasn't.

Hen decided to fill the remainder of the day with mundane tasks to get her mind off of Georgie and hidden cameras and theft and police stations. She took Lilly on a trip to the grocery store. It always took ten times as long to buy groceries with Lilly in tow, however, Hen was glad for the distraction today. As Lilly kicked her legs feverishly in the cart, Hen could see she was getting bored and decided to make things more exciting. She lined up the cart in front of an empty aisle and began to run down as fast as she could, pushing the cart and making car noises. Hen turned to the left with a jolt once they reached the end and made screechy brake noises, loud enough to be fun, but not so loud to annoy all the other shoppers.

"And Lilly wins! Photo finish!" Hen called out in a whisper-shout. Lilly giggled uncontrollably in excitement.

"More! More!" she pleaded.

"Okay, okay, just one more time," Hen agreed.

She got the race-car, or grocery cart for those without a toddler's imagination, into position and began to race once again down the aisle. Unfortunately, a large man wearing a suit and hat made the corner just as Lilly's car was about to screech past the finish line. Hen nearly bowled him over but was able to turn out of the way in time.

"Oh, my goodness, I'm so sorry! We didn't see you there." Hen explained.

"Humph," the man grumbled and promptly turned away hiding his face.

Hen kept her mouth shut while she pushed Lilly and the cart slowly away until they were out of earshot of the man.

"Oopsies!" she said to Lilly, giggling along with her toddler.

The two finished their grocery shopping and headed home with Hen feeling much better about the earlier events of the day. Time with Lilly often seemed to do that. There was a magic about her. She just had a way of making people happy, especially on the days Hen needed it most. Hen was glad to have the whole Mrs. Nettles and Georgie situation behind her.

She unclipped her daughter from the car-seat and lugged a sleepy Lilly, along with a few bags of groceries, like a pack-mule to the front door. She placed her daughter down and began to unlock the door when Lilly grabbed something up off the welcome mat.

"Mommy!" she said, holding it up proudly. In Lilly's tiny fingers was a small, yellowed envelope. On it, Hen's full first name was written in the same loopy calligraphy that she had become so familiar with. 'Henrietta' had received another letter from Mrs. Nettles.

CHAPTER FIFTEEN

Hen placed the envelope on the counter and put the groceries away before Lilly could get into anything. She made the two of them a late pasta dinner, taking her time to cut up all the noodles for Lilly and cut up some fresh basil to garnish her own helping. She put extra bubbles in the bath for Lilly, read more books than usual at bedtime until her daughter couldn't keep her eyes open any longer, ran the vacuum sweeper after Lilly had fallen asleep, organized her junk drawer and dusted between the keys on her computer. In fact, Hen did just about everything *except* read Mrs. Nettles letter.

After making herself a cup of tea and putting on her pajamas, Hen walked around the house shutting off the lights and locking the doors. Before flipping the switch in the kitchen, she glanced interminably at the envelope on the counter, but eventually turned the light off and walked upstairs with only her tea in hand.

She made her way to her lonely bedroom and sat up under her covers for a while responding to a few text messages. She told Harry that everything was fine and nothing much was going on except for finding a new park that she and Lilly both enjoyed going to. *No reason to worry him or distract him from all that he has going on.* Thinking about it for a moment, she could literally be in Timbuktu and Harry would have no idea as long as she responded to texts and answered his phone calls every so often. She hadn't planned to keep things from him, it just worked out that way. Now that she had, she wasn't really sure how to go back and explain, so she just didn't.

Hen finished her tea, brushed her teeth, and crawled back under the covers, but her eyes were wide open. The curiosity was killing her. She couldn't avoid it any longer. Hen had to open that letter.

She bolted back to the kitchen on tiptoe, snagged the letter, and then ran back to her spot under the blankets on her bed. Something about receiving this newest correspondence from beyond the grave was more unnerving, now that Hen knew that Mrs. Nettles knew real secrets about a real person. What more could the old woman have to say? Hen turned her bedside lamp on brighter and pulled her covers up over her as a layer of protection, then finally slid her index finger under the seal and opened the envelope. Perhaps it was just a result of old age, but the adhesion of the envelope flap was particularly fragile, almost as if it had already been opened.

The card itself was definitely from the same stationery set. This one had a little boy on it, running with a pig under his arm. *What is it with nursery rhymes and pigs?* Hen opened it and quietly read its message aloud:

Henrietta,

Consider the art of stealing. It is indeed an art, requiring precision and dedication. As what some might call a woman of means, I have plenty of experience with thieves. Only the smart ones ever succeed. Is stealing a crime? We must be the judge. Who is he stealing from? What has he taken? I, myself, am guilty of stealing the spotlight. I am grateful to have had my heart stolen away. So, we must ask ourselves: what and how and from whom. Must it always be a crime?

Mrs. Nettles

"What the heck does any of that mean?" Hen asked herself aloud. *She must be referring to Georgie and how he stole from her, probably during those visits to her house. She knew he was selling stolen goods. But why the cryptic text?*

Hen shrugged off her own question and went to put the card back in its envelope. Though, try as she might, it kept getting stuck. She reached her hand into the envelope to open it up a bit more and realized that there was another piece of paper inside. It was torn, but Hen recognized the ivy on the border and immediately identified it as a sheet of Nettles stationery. The black ink wasn't the loopy cursive of Mrs. Nettles. The message was written in a swift, messy script, like one might expect of a doctor's hand:

Henrietta,

You have solved the riddle of Georgie Porgie, might you also of Tom?

Hen quickly flicked the scrap of paper onto the floor like it was a spider and pulled her covers around her haphazardly. How could anyone have possibly known that she was involved with the collection of evidence against Georgie? Was someone following her?

She closed her eyes and breathed deeply. *Calm down, Hen.* Leaning out of bed, she grabbed the corner of the now crumpled paper. Hen held it delicately from the very corner, as if it were about to bite her.

Without realizing it, Hen found herself making another list. She *could* deduce the following:

1. Mrs. Nettles did not write the addendum to the original notecard.
2. Someone knew that she was receiving mail from Mrs. Nettles, that Mrs. Nettles had sent her clues about Georgie, and that Hen had been involved in convicting him.

3. The same someone used a piece of Nettles stationery to write a note to her, but either strategically or coincidentally tore off the portion of the page where the Nettles name appeared.

Hen *could not* answer the following burning questions:

1. Who was this mystery writer with the sloppy handwriting?
2. What did they have to gain from contacting her?
3. Were they sending her all of the mail she had received so far or were they just using their knowledge of Mrs. Nettles' correspondence to their advantage?
4. Who in the world was Tom?
5. What was Hen to do about all this?

That last one puzzled her most. At the very least, someone was watching her. Was it safe to involve herself further in Mrs. Nettles' affairs? Hen looked back at the notecard. She hadn't the foggiest idea what Mrs. Nettles was talking about. All that talk of stealing and theft…had someone else stolen from the woman? If Hen chose to continue untangling these riddles, where would she even begin to get started?

She held up the piece of ripped paper. How had this mystery writer ended up with a piece of this personalized stationery? Where would it have come from? After a brief moment of consideration, the answer came to Hen without a doubt. The Nettles Mansion.

CHAPTER SIXTEEN

Hen leaned heavily against her trusty silver minivan as she held the gas pump in one hand and a lousy, extremely hot cup of gas station coffee in the other. On some days, she was sure that she was a morning person, and on other days, like today, she was very sure that she was not. Having dropped off Lilly at her mom's house near the crack of dawn and having hardly slept at all the past two nights, Hen was beyond exhausted.

Her mom had agreed to watch Lilly only if Hen was able to come first thing that morning since her driveway was being repaved.

"That's no problem!" Hen had said. She was regretting that response now.

Hen glanced up at the dimly lit screen on the pump. The numbers just kept going up and up. It had only been a few minutes since she pulled in, but it felt like she had been standing there dumping gas into her tank for ages. There were two things that minivans don't have going for them. First, they guzzle up gas, no matter how fuel efficient they claim to be, and second, they do not, and will not ever, look cool. Hen had accepted these truths a long time ago when she happily traded in her archaic sedan for something with trunk space, air-conditioning, and power windows. *The lap of luxury.*

The nozzle clicked off and Hen paid for her full tank. She tried once again to take a sip of the coffee and burnt her tongue a second time.

Placing it in the cupholder, she plugged the address of Nettles Mansion back into her GPS and drove off.

A trip to the gas station was never convenient, but the last thing she wanted was to run out of gas on those winding roads in the middle of the forest, or worse, once she'd reached the mansion itself.

The plan was to simply knock on the door and see if anyone answered. Someone had to be inhabiting the mansion and that someone wrote her a note. Hopefully, she could speak with a living, breathing human about some of the questions that had been on her mind. If she got any creepy vibes, she would just get right back in the car and leave. She would not accept an invitation to enter the mansion. Not yet, anyway. She would just talk to Mr. or Mrs. Note-writer in the doorway. *IF they answered the door...and that was a big "if".*

It wasn't the most elaborate plan, but it was all she had to go on. Hen turned up the music on the stereo. It was refreshing to listen to her own CDs every now and again instead of Lilly's. Who knows, maybe someday, she'll be able to choose the channel on the television again. Someday.

She turned off the highway onto the first of many winding roads, each one skinnier than the last. Hen was hopeful that she would not pass a car going the opposite direction on those goat paths.

She began to think through what she might say upon her arrival. Should she introduce herself with her real name? Probably not. Maybe she should wait to see if they knew who she was prior to her telling them. That would confirm their involvement in some way with the letters and the note she received.

Before she could plan out much more, a slapping sound from the front right of her car interrupted her thoughts. The minivan started to vibrate unsteadily. She decelerated and held tight to the steering wheel as she fought to continue driving straight forward on the road until pulling off onto the side of the road as best she could, despite the lack of a proper shoulder.

"What in the world?" Hen yelled once she gained a bit of composure. She turned off the ignition and stepped out to see what was going on. It was immediately obvious. She was no car aficionado, but she could identify a flat tire. *Crap.*

Hen kicked the tire, then instantly regretted it. *Tires are pretty stinking hard for being made out of rubber.* Walking around to the back of the car and opening the trunk, she rummaged around for longer than it should have required as she searched for a spare tire. Hen sighed, finally remembering where to find it: under her pile of stuff that had accumulated in the trunk, hidden in that secret compartment thing they make nearly invisible to stupid people who are stranded on the side of the road. *Okay, you've got this Hen.* She lugged it out and was proud of herself for a moment for remembering to grab the tire iron as well. She walked over to the deflated, sad tire and looked at it for a while, holding a heavier-than-she-would-have-thought spare and a big metal stick she had no idea what to do with. Why didn't she know how to change a tire? She felt completely helpless.

After standing there staring like an idiot for a who knows how long, Hen opened the driver's side door and sat back down to think. *Okay, so maybe you don't got this. Just be an adult. Just call someone.* Hen grabbed her phone and crossed her fingers that she had service. She was beyond relieved to see a few bars of service in the upper corner. *Thank goodness.*

She looked up tow trucks in the area and called the only one close enough to be listed. Unfortunately, they didn't answer, and she didn't feel like waiting around until they did. Next, Hen texted her mom to explain that she might be later than planned. No response there either. Finally, she pulled up the contact for her regular mechanic, thankful to already have the number programmed in her phone. It would probably be a fortune to get them to drive all the way out to meet her, but at least she wouldn't be stuck on the side of the road alone.

By some miracle, they agreed to send someone out within the next hour or so. Hen sighed deeply and sat with her head leaning back against the headrest. Today was turning out to be a less-than-great day. At least her coffee had finally cooled off. Hen did her best to relax, listening to the rest of the CDs hidden away in the glove box and drinking the gas station brew.

After what seemed like hours but was really about forty minutes, a tow-truck pulled up behind her.

"Hey there!" a man called out, beeping his horn.

Hen waved back at him out the window sheepishly. The truck driver pulled off a considerable distance behind Hen and began to saunter over. She recognized him at once. It was Not-Tom.

He must have also recognized her. Quickening his pace when their eyes met, he shouted, "Henrietta Mrs.-Not-Miss Bellemore!" Hen could tell that he was trying to make up for getting flustered after she corrected him during their last conversation. She controlled the urge to roll her eyes.

"Yep…" Hen meant to continue by saying 'and you are…' but she realized that she had completely forgotten his real name. All she knew was that his name was not Tom. Luckily, it didn't matter because Not-Tom was in a talkative mood.

"Oh man, we are way out here, aren't we? No one ever drives these old roads. I honestly don't even know if they maintain 'em. I just 'bout ran over a downed tree a mile back. No guard rails out here or nothin'. Now if I was 'bout to work on this road, I would just start with…"

He continued on but Hen was far too tired and uninterested to keep listening to Not-Tom expound upon road maintenance. Her mind drifted back to the note that had led her toward Nettles Mansion in the first place. Why had the anonymous sender decided to include it? Perhaps so she knew that someone was keeping tabs on her? Did they want her to solve the next puzzle or were they hoping that she would scare off? Why even mention Georgie and…

"TOM!" she shouted, interrupting Not-Tom's story about how he used to hate driving on these old roads way back when.

"Whoa there, woman!" he retorted, demonstrably startled.

"Sorry," Hen said, slightly embarrassed.

"It's Gene by the way," he replied.

"Oh, yeah, I know," Hen said quickly, although she really didn't. "I was just thinking about how you said you had worked with a guy named Tom."

"Yeah?" Gene furrowed his brow in confusion as he waited for Hen to continue.

"Yeah. I have been looking for someone named Tom and I was wondering if maybe it was the same guy."

"Tom Wilson?" Gene asked.

"Um…maybe? I'm not sure of his last name."

"You're lookin' for a guy named Tom, but you don't know his last name."

"Right."

"Well, what's he look like?"

Hen bit her bottom lip for a moment, "Well, you see, I don't really know."

"'Ya don't know what he looks like or what his last name is but you're looking for a guy with the most common name since Joe."

Hen hesitated for a moment and finally admitted, "Yes."

Gene's brow resumed its furrow, "I'm not really sure if I can help 'ya. There's a buncha' Tom's out there. Why do 'ya wanna find him anyways?" Hen sighed. He was probably right.

"I just thought it might be a coincidence or something." She looked down a bit dejected.

"They do exist, 'ya know. It is a small world. Tell 'ya what, I'll see if I can call up old Tom. His number's probably around the shop somewhere. I'll tell him you're looking for him."

"Oh, that's great!" Hen replied, "Except you don't have to tell him it's me. I'm actually just trying to get in touch with him for a friend."

"Oh, okay." Gene paused for a moment. "Then what should I tell him?"

Hen thought for a few seconds and responded, "How about asking if he knew Mrs. Nettles?"

"*The* Mrs. Nettles?"

"Mmm-hmm," Hen said while she pursed her lips, trying desperately not to give too much away.

"Well, gee. That's the small world I was just talking 'bout. The one my cousin and I used to work for when we took these old roads out here all those years ago."

Hen was taken aback, "Wait, you knew her?"

"Well, not really. I only helped out now and then, but Derry, gosh, he kept in touch with her for a long time."

Hen's heart started to beat a little faster. Perhaps she wasn't figuratively at a dead-end after all. Literally though, she was still sitting on the side of the road in a car with a flat tire.

"Is Derry still around here?" she asked as calmly as she could muster.

"Well yeah. We talked about him last time you came into the shop." Hen paused to recall their previous conversation.

"You mean Derrick Tittle?"

"The very same," Gene replied.

Hen couldn't quite think of what to ask next. From what she had seen and heard Derrick Tittle was pretty popular around town. How was she supposed to sit down and talk with him?

She opened her mouth to ask Gene that very question but he was already checking out the front right wheel of her minivan. Hen opened the door and hopped out of the car herself.

"'Ya know, it'd be a waste of money to have me tow 'ya. Your car here's just got a flat tire. Want me to change it for 'ya?"

Hen felt her face flush. She hated being offered help almost as much as she hated asking for it, but she swallowed her pride this time.

"That would be great."

After he had finished the embarrassingly quick job of changing her flat, Gene put back her tire iron and threw her old tire in his truck.

"Why don't 'ya stop by the shop sometime and I'll fix 'ya up with a new tire."

"That sounds great," Hen answered bashfully. "I guess you can't really fix tires, huh?"

Gene laughed, "Well, not ones like this! You have a handful of nails in there." He paused for a moment and looked down. "Actually..." Gene walked a few paces back and brushed his hand along the ground. "I'm glad I parked back there. There's a box full of nails dumped on the ground here." Hen looked around. They were in the middle of the forest. Why were there so many nails dumped in the middle of the road? Gene's eyes met Hen's as he verbalized what they were both thinking, "It's almost like they were put here on purpose."

CHAPTER SEVENTEEN

Hen wasn't self-important enough to assume this likely road trap was laid especially for her. However, it seemed clear that someone was trying to make the way to Nettles Mansion difficult. She and her minivan could attest to that.

Gene had been incredibly helpful, not only with the flat tire, but also with his connection to Mrs. Nettles. He agreed to ask if his cousin would be willing to talk with Hen, though he was not confident in the reply she would receive. Interestingly enough, Gene thought he might even have some of the old files that Derrick Tittle had left him in a box from his old business.

"Believe it or not, the near-famous Derrick Tittle once owned a small cleaning and repair company fixin' up old clocks and maintaining all those little trinkets. Mrs. Nettles had 'bout a million of 'em. He was always fixin' up something of hers," Gene explained. "I tagged along and cleaned up the workspace when he needed me. Sometimes I'd hand him some tiny tool. I never quite got the itch to fix up old watches and record players, but give me a car any day."

While Hen hoped he did find more information, at least knowing what Mrs. Nettles deemed important enough to have fixed could give her some insight about the inside of the mansion and perhaps even about the woman herself.

"So which way 'ya headed?" Gene asked as Hen returned to her car.

"I probably need to go home. My mom's watching Lilly and it's already been longer than I initially expected."

"Well, that's good then," Gene replied. "I wouldn't want 'ya bumpin' around on those roads ahead much further on your spare."

"Oh right." Hen mused as that hadn't even occurred to her. "Will I be okay to get home?"

"Yeah, you'll be good. Tell 'ya what, stop in tomorrow if you're free and I'll get 'ya all sorted out at the shop. I'll be there all day."

Hen was really glad to have had her regular mechanic shop's number in her phone. Gene was really growing on her.

"I can't thank you enough," she said truthfully.

"Eh, no worries. It's my job."

After a short pause, Hen broke the silence, "Well, I'd better get going so I can pick up Lilly before it gets much later."

"That's right. It's nice having someone to get home to," Gene replied softly. Hen thought on his words. At first, she wasn't sure if he was trying to hint at something or hit on her, but she quickly realized that he was simply saying exactly what he meant. Hen hoped that Gene had someone to go home to, though his slightly poignant expression led her to assume otherwise.

"Yeah," Hen said gently.

Back to his chipper self, Gene cheerfully remarked, "Well, take care, 'ya hear?"

"Same to you," Hen replied and watched as Gene hopped back into his truck. She attempted a three-point turn, which turned into more of a seven-point turn by the end of it and drove back the way she had come.

Hen felt a little sorry for Gene. There were times, when Harry was away, that she had thrown pity parties for herself, fighting the misery of loneliness. However, she wasn't really alone, not even in those moments. She had her favorite person in the world to keep her company. As Lilly was growing up, Hen grew to love her more and more. She gave Lilly the biggest, squishiest hug when she picked her up, feeling more thankful than ever to have her sweet girl to come home to.

Then, after oohing and aahing over the new pavement in her mom's driveway for longer than she really cared to, Hen drove home. She and Lilly played in the yard and picked wildflowers, which were mostly weeds that had gotten out of control, though Lilly didn't seem to mind. For a few hours, Hen pushed the worries from her mind and searched for little bugs in the grass, laid on a blanket, ate peanut butter and jelly, and appreciated the simple and wonder-filled perspective on life from her one-and-a-half-year-old.

At the end of the day, Lilly gave her mom the gift of a peaceful and early bedtime, so Hen found herself with two free hands and a little extra time. She decided to tidy her trunk since realizing it was a mess from the whole ordeal earlier in the day. Out came toys, wrappers, empty bottles that she had meant to take to recycling, a box of clothes that she had meant to drop off at the thrift store, and not one or two, but six umbrellas.

She laid it all out on the ground and sorted the lot, putting most things back into the car but swearing to actually drop them off like she had originally planned. Along with a bag of garbage and five umbrellas, Hen flung the bag that held a few of Mrs. Nettles books and her case file over her arm and took everything inside.

Cozying up on the couch with a blanket, Hen found herself leafing back through the case file. There was no mention of a man named Tom, but she did reexamine the remaining two drawings that she had determined were maps, like the one of the antique store bathroom.

Hen couldn't really make out what either drawing was supposed to be. The first was a bunch of rectangles with a few numbers and an 'x'.

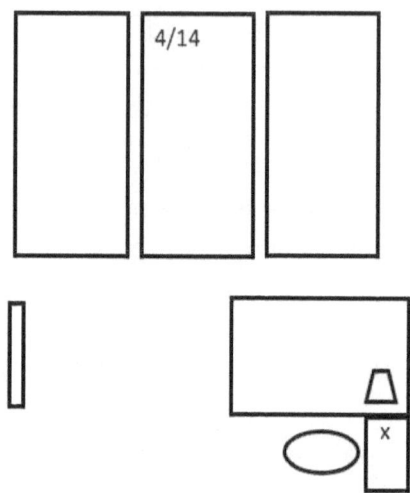

Hen was baffled. She pondered on the inclusion of numbers in this particular drawing. What was 4/14 referring to? Could it be a fraction? If so, why not simplify to 2/7? Or perhaps it was a measurement...was she supposed to be looking for something that was four inches wide by fourteen inches long? Hen thought back to the first of the drawings that hadn't made sense until she knew exactly to what it was referring. She supposed that these last two were going to also remain a puzzle until more pieces fell into place.

The last drawing was even more confusing, just a series of boxes.

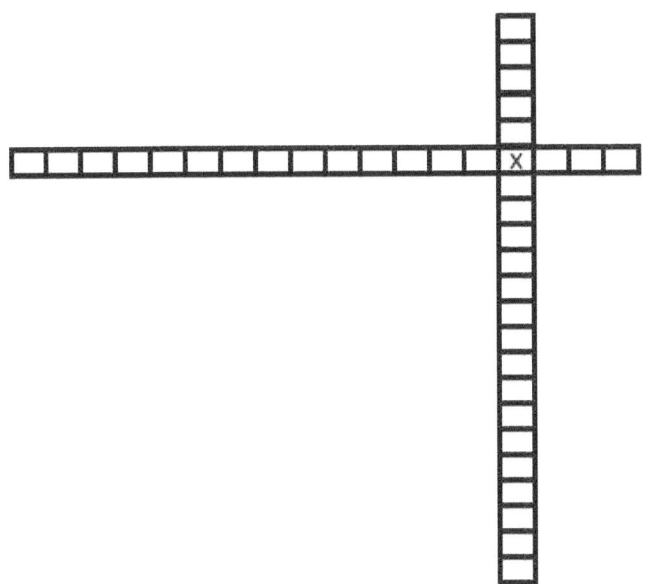

There were no numbers, no other shapes. It looked to Hen like a very boring empty crossword puzzle. Flipping the drawing over, she discovered two words: "Straight-Wait". *Oh, well that clears it up,* Hen thought to herself sarcastically.

She decided to move on from the drawings since she didn't seem to be getting anywhere. Hen placed the case file beside her on the couch and grabbed the illustrations book. A thought came to her. She had never figured out what nursery rhyme was being referenced in the illustration on her last card from Mrs. Nettles. She had been so distracted by the additional note inside that she had forgotten to examine the significance of the card itself.

Hen cracked the spine and began leafing through the pages. None of the images seemed familiar. When she reached about the halfway mark, she got an idea. Hen flipped back to the table of contents to read the titles for a certain name. There was not just one rhyme, but three that contained the name 'Tom' in the title: "Tom Thumb",

"Little Tommy Tucker", and "Tom, Tom the Piper's Son". *Gene was right. Tom is a common name.*

After a few more page turns, recognition rang as Hen looked at a squealing pig under the arm of what she now could confirm was Tom the piper's son. She looked up the words to the rhyme and read them over a few times.

Tom, Tom, the piper's son

Stole a pig, and away did run

The pig was eat

And Tom was beat

So Tom went howling down the street

Of course! Tom was, in fact, referring to a nursery rhyme character and not a real person, Hen thought, gently smacking her palm to her forehead. Now she just needed to figure out who…liked bacon a lot? Hen laughed out loud at that thought. That's probably not quite what Mrs. Nettles meant.

CHAPTER EIGHTEEN

"You found him?" Gene's eyebrows raised so high in surprise that he looked like an animated character.

Hen only nodded in response, not wanting to explain the details of why she was looking for Tom in the first place.

"Of all the Toms in all the world. You know what I think, that's fate there."

"Perhaps," Hen said with a smile, bumping Lilly up a bit on her hip. "It might also have been fate that I ended up calling the shop yesterday. Thanks again. Seriously."

"All in a day's work ma'am," Gene replied in a chipper tone. Hen appreciated the sentiment, but she knew that Gene had really gone above and beyond 'a day's work'. He not only saved her money by fixing her flat yesterday, but also made sure that her tires were replaced and she could once again drive her car safely. "I'll get this finished up right quick and you'll be good to go," Gene said kindly.

"Awesome. And thank you…again," Hen replied. She was still a bit embarrassed to accept help, but humble enough to realize that she really needed it sometimes.

"Here 'ya go." Gene gave her a slip of paper for the service. "And *here* 'ya go." He dropped a big cardboard box on the counter between them.

Hen inspected the box before her. Outside, it displayed a Mr. Wrench logo, complete with a cartoon wrench with eyes and a mouth smiling at her. Beneath Mr. Wrench, a tagline read, "We'll Find What You Need to Fix It."

"Is this for me?" Hen asked, confused. She held Lilly's hand back from touching the box, as it was covered in dust and what she assumed were greasy fingerprints.

"Well, not to keep," Gene replied. "I hold on to all this kinda' stuff in case I need it someday, 'ya know?"

Hen nodded her head in acknowledgement, but the look of confusion remained on her face as she glanced at the slightly disturbing Mr. Wrench cartoon.

Gene saw her gaze and seemed to catch on, "Oh!" he laughed, "No, it's not car parts! It's papers, see?"

He tilted the open box toward her while Hen got on her tiptoes and peered inside. She was slightly shocked to find a sea of manilla folders and important-looking papers haphazardly thrown together. Hen was beginning to feel better about the state of her messy trunk.

"If there ever was a log-book or somethin' from Derry's, 'er I mean, *Derrick's* tinkerin' days, it'd be here."

"Oh right. Thank you!" Hen was not particularly looking forward to sorting Gene's mess of papers but was legitimately excited to learn more about Mrs. Nettles' belongings.

Once she and Lilly returned home from the mechanic's shop later that day, Hen tried to distract her daughter with toys, play doh, and even turned on the television, but Lilly wasn't having it. Nothing looked as fun as Hen's box full of papers.

"Are you sure you don't want to play with dollies?" Hen coaxed.

"No no no no no," Lilly replied. *Well, that was clear.*

Now realizing that Lilly wouldn't be satisfied unless she explored the contents of the box, Hen switched gears, "Okay, you can help me sort through these." Lilly's eyes lit up. Sometimes, the most mundane things were the ones that excited her most. "But we have to use gentle hands. These are important. Okay?"

Lilly smiled up at her, seemingly understanding. Hen never quite knew just how much Lilly picked up on, but she had learned not to underestimate her.

Hen paused to set up a kind of sorting game. She placed two baskets on the ground and designated them accordingly:

Pink Basket: Important- Might be pertinent to Mrs. Nettles/Hen

Yellow Basket: Not Important- Definitely not of interest to her

The *game* consisted of Hen glancing at a piece of paper from the Mr. Wrench box and telling Lilly what color basket to put it in. Hen had strategically picked pink and yellow because they were the two colors Lilly knew so far.

It was probably the most boring game in the world to anyone else, but Hen watched as her daughter eagerly placed each piece of paper (with gentle hands no less!) into the correct basket. Each time she ran back giggling as she awaited the next sheet. Hen recalled all the activities she had tried to plan for Lilly that had required far more set up and had been less successful than this.

They continued to play the sorting game for a good twenty minutes before Hen realized the box was nearly empty. Dishearteningly, almost all of the papers had made their way into the yellow basket. She had tossed a few nearly illegible ones into the pink, along with a big packet of numbers that was unlabeled, but nothing that specifically mentioned any work having been done at the Nettles Mansion.

"Snack!" Lilly chirped, noticing the pause in the game.

"Alright, let's go to the kitchen," replied Hen, grateful for a break. She felt weariness in her eyes from reading all of that tiny text. "What are you in the mood for? Blueberries?"

"Boobers," Lilly confirmed. Hen began to put the blueberries in a bowl, but when she opened the fridge, Lilly caught a glimpse inside.

"No no no!" She shook her head when her mom tried to hand her a bowl full of exactly what she asked for.

"Not blueberries?" Hen asked patiently.

"No."

"Okay, what do you want instead?"

"Cheese! Cheese!" Lilly called out.

"Just a minute, Lilly Billy. Let me cut it up for you." Hen put the berries back in the fridge and put cheese cubes in the bowl instead. Lilly smiled ear to ear. *It must be so satisfying when others start to understand you as you learn to communicate,* Hen ruminated to herself.

Hen, on the other hand, wasn't feeling very satisfied in her own project. She finished up sorting what remained in the box and ended up with a yellow basket filled to the brim with old receipts for car parts, and notes about who had stopped into the shop and what they had worked on. The pink basket held a few pieces of paper that seemed irrelevant but also weren't specifically related to the mechanic's shop. This pile included the unmarked file folder filled with a list of numbers, a business card for Derrick Tittle and Co., Handyman and Horologist, and a pocket-sized notebook.

Hen's excitement grew as she flipped through the notebook's first ten pages or so which listed customers of the repair business and the items that had been repaired, but none of the customers listed were Mrs. Nettles. In fact, none of the names had been familiar to Hen and none of the items had seemed out of the ordinary. She did notice a few numbers listed by each name, though. *Order numbers perhaps?* After these first few pages, the rest of the notebook was blank.

Hen sighed. Given that she was not an accountant and definitely not a businessperson either, she was going to have to seek assistance…again.

Who did she know that could decipher all these numbers? Preferably someone knowledgeable in the business world, yet relatively uninformed on the goings-on of the Nettles Mansion. She paused to think. Did she even know any accountants or businessmen?

Hen thought for far too long before she guiltily realized she was married to one.

CHAPTER NINETEEN

Hen couldn't believe that she had forgotten that Harry worked in the field. Before she could talk herself out of it, she sent a text to Harry asking if he could help with "a business question" because she was "figuring something out for a friend." After having already sent it, she read back her words and cringed a bit. He was going to be at very least confused, or worse immediately suspicious.

Why had she been so careful to keep Mrs. Nettles and all the goings on from her husband? Did she truly not want to worry him? Or was she feeling guilty for her involvement in the first place? The more invested she became, the harder it would be to tell him. *Yeah, but it's easier not to get him involved,* she reasoned as she decided once again to leave him as in the dark as possible.

"Cookie!" Lilly shouted excitedly from across the room.

"I don't think we have any," Hen replied honestly, remembering that she had finished off her secret cookie stash a few days ago.

"Cookie! Cookie! Mama...cookie?" Lilly looked up with her big, beautiful eyes. Hen melted like a stick of butter, just like the one that she found herself grabbing from the fridge, along with a few eggs and some flour from the pantry.

"Okay, you little stinker. We can make some cookies. Chocolate chip or oatmeal?"

"Eeee!" Lilly squealed, too exuberant to answer in words.

"So… chocolate chip?" Hen shrugged.

Lilly looked up at her mom for a minute in seeming contemplation, "Chip!" she answered definitively.

"Alright then." Hen and Lilly got to work, washing their hands and measuring out the baking ingredients, even getting a few in the mixing bowl.

Just as the dough started to reach its stickiest stage, Lilly lunged forward, reaching in with both hands. Her small palms were completely coated in dough as she grabbed Hen's hands and pulled them into the bowl as well. Hen laughed at the two of them transforming into a sweet, sticky mess!

"Hmm, might as well," Hen said as she and Lilly dumped the half-full bag of chocolate chips into the bowl and began to mix it together with their bare hands.

Hen's phone could be heard ringing in the adjacent room.

"They are going to have to wait a sec," she commented to Lilly and continued mixing. Soon after, she thought she heard it again. Then again. "What is going on?" she wondered aloud. Though Hen was anxious to check her phone, she became immediately distracted by the task at hand, trying to keep Lilly from tossing all the leftover flour onto the floor and failing miserably.

Having placed the cookies on a baking sheet in the oven and fully scrubbed her daughter, her kitchen, and herself, Hen finally made her way over to see who had tried to get in touch with her. Alerts for two missed calls and several texts lit up her phone.

Notifications of missed calls from Abby and Harry along with four texts and no voicemails. Hen was glad for that, no one has time for voicemails anymore. She read through the texts:

From Abby:

"Hey Hen. Are you mad at me? I haven't heard back from you recently. I miss you. I want to give you space if that's what you need, but I just saw the news about the arrest. That's crazy! Were you involved? Please text me back."

A pang of guilt ran through Hen's body because she really had been avoiding Abby since she accused Hen of putting Lilly in danger. Hen knew Abby was right, she had even taken her friend's advice, but that didn't mean she had quite forgiven her yet. It brought her back to when Abby had moved away. Hen was embarrassed to admit it now, but it had taken her a long time before she finally forgave Abby for leaving. Abby was just as annoyingly understanding back then too. It made Hen feel like an awful person for needing so much time to process and forgive.

But what was that she had said about the news? Abby knew that Hen didn't watch the local news. *What was she talking about? Who got arrested?*

From Harry:

"Hey. I called but missed you. What did you need help with?"

Very direct and to the point. The most business-y of businessmen, even in a text to his wife. He wasn't always that direct or distant. It came out more when he was around his colleagues or associates, which always made Hen feel uncomfortable. Actually, he was quite funny and lighthearted when he was actually home. Hen missed that. She pondered on how much Harry had changed in recent years. He used to be goofy and silly most of the time. She was the one asking him to take things more seriously. Now though, Hen missed that goofy side of him.

From Tammy:

"Oh. My. Gosh. We did it! I can't believe they have Mr. Brown in custody. Can you believe it?! I kind of want both of us to get the credit, but I think you're right…it's better that we're anonymous. Anyway, just wanted to say thanks. I feel a lot safer now. And also vindicated. What a creep. It was fun being a spy with you! Let me know when you want to do it again! Or, you know, just go to get coffee together or something! Love you girl!"

Whoa. Georgie is actually paying for his crimes. Hen wasn't sure what she was expecting when she'd dropped off the evidence at the police station, but she had a pit in her stomach at the thought of her actions actually sending someone to jail. It was a feeling she hadn't seen coming. Superheroes in movies never feel bad for getting the bad guy. Why did she?

Hen didn't think of herself as a hero. She felt relieved that Georgie wasn't taking footage of his employees getting undressed in the bathroom. She was glad that he wasn't stealing from any more old ladies. And yet, she felt odd. The burden of responsibility that his arrest resulted directly from her actions weighed heavily on her shoulders.

For the first time, Hen felt a bit like a pawn in Mrs. Nettles' game. Though, it wasn't a game. This was reality, and, whether or not he deserved it, a man's life was forever changed for the worse because of her.

Before Hen could check the last text, she heard the high-pitched timer go off in the kitchen and ran in to check on the cookies. The familiar scent of buttery brown sugar and gooey chocolate was comforting at a time like this. She pulled out the tray. *Mmm…Perfect.* If she could do nothing else, at least she could bake a good batch of chocolate chip cookies.

Hen tossed a few in the refrigerator knowing that Lilly wouldn't be able to wait for them to cool off at room temperature. Hen glanced over at her daughter as she piled the pillows from the couch onto the floor and performed a big belly flop on top of them. Lilly giggled, brushed her hair out of her eyes, and flopped again, bursting into more laughter.

Hen laughed quietly to herself at her little goofball and took the free moment to respond to the messages on her phone. As she picked it up, her phone went off in her hand displaying another message from Harry.

"A business question huh? Okay shoot."

He must be done with his workday. He sounds a lot less professional now.

"Yeah. I have this packet of numbers and I'm not really sure what it is or what it means."

"Hmm, could you send me a picture of it?"

Hen snapped some photos of the packet from Gene's box and sent them to Harry. She was a bit surprised at how he was immediately willing to help. Maybe she should give him a little more credit. Maybe she could share that she could use more help at home.

116

That thought made her feel instantly guilty. After a minute or two, the phone rang with a call from Harry.

"Hey Harry. Any luck?"

"Hen, who is this friend? Are you close with them?"

"What? No, not really. I'm just um...sorting some old paperwork as a favor for someone. I didn't know what stack that belonged in." Hen was getting better at telling the truth, but not the whole truth.

"Well, I hate to tell you this, but I think your friend is embezzling funds."

"Wait, really?" Hen replied in disbelief. Did Gene know about this? It seemed highly unlikely that it would be him since he so freely handed her a box containing something incriminating.

"Yeah. And they kept track of each amount that they stole in great detail. Who does that?"

"How can you be sure?" Hen asked. "It just looks like a bunch of columns of numbers to me."

"I'm pretty sure. It even keeps track of money sent to 'personal account'. Pretty stupid."

"Is there any way to figure out what business this is?"

"Well, it's a 501C3," Harry retorted. Hen waited for him to explain, which he didn't.

"So... that means... what exactly?" she finally asked.

"It's a non-profit. I really think you ought to report this," Harry answered.

"To who? I don't even really know whose it is."

"Isn't it your friend's?" Harry inquired.

"Hmm. It was in the stuff he gave me to sort but I'm not sure who it belongs to. Maybe I'll...ask him first?"

"I would. As long as you are sure he's not involved."

"I'm pretty sure," Hen replied.

After a long beat, Harry said softly, "Hen, are you ok? Maybe I should just look into it. I'm not crazy about you being involved in a scandal." Hen was immediately thankful that she hadn't told Harry about Georgie.

"I'm good, really. I'll just ask him about it."

"Okay…" Harry sounded skeptical, "but, wha-"

"Hey, do you want to talk to Lilly Billy?" Hen interrupted as she clumsily changed the subject. There was a slight pause.

"I'd love to."

Hen smiled and handed over the phone to Lilly who gleefully conversed with her dad in her own adorable way.

After she had hung up, Hen glanced down at the screen to realize that she still had one unread text notification. A lump formed in her throat as she read.

From an unknown number:

"Stop getting involved in what doesn't concern you, Henrietta Bellemore."

CHAPTER TWENTY

Hen stared at the phone screen for a long while. The message itself wasn't exactly a threat, but it also was certainly unfriendly. What's more, the idea that someone not only knew what she was up to but also her personal phone number sent a chill down her spine. Hen held the phone in her hand, deciding on whether or not to reply. If she did, the sender would know they indeed had the right number, but if she didn't, would she regret not asking who it was and perhaps acquiring more answers.

She eventually decided that the former would be safer than the latter, so she hastily blocked the number and threw her phone in her purse. She needed it out of sight and out of mind for a little while.

Lilly ran over and began to tug on Hen's pant leg.

"What's up, babe?" Hen asked her.

"Book, Mama," Lilly responded. Hen smiled. Toddlerhood was tough sometimes, but it was so wonderful when Lilly could actually tell her what she wanted. She didn't have to play the guessing game of figuring it out all the time.

"Okay! Let's read a book." Hen walked over to the bookshelf and pulled out a compilation of princess stories.

"No, no." Lilly shook her head.

"Not a princess story? You sure?" Hen coaxed.

"No," Lilly replied definitively.

"Okay…" Hen grabbed another book with a penguin on the cover.

"No, no." Lilly shook her head again. So much for avoiding the guessing game.

"No penguins either?"

"No penwin."

"Hmm, okay, what do you want then?"

"Apple," Lilly said.

"Oh, are you hungry? Do you want a snack?"

"No, no, no!" Lilly stomped her feet this time.

Hen took a deep sigh. They were both getting a little frustrated.

"Help me out here, Lilly Babe. Do you want to still read a book?"

Lilly nodded. "Apple," she said again.

Hen finally realized that Lilly was trying to say that she wanted to read a book about apples. She searched up and down the bookshelf to no avail. *Do we even have a book with apples in it?*

"Mama. Apples." Lilly tugged at her mom's hand and pointed to Hen's bag by the door. Hen opened it up and sure enough, a tattered old cover caught her eye: A was an Apple Pie. Hen had almost forgotten about the book that started it all.

She began to read to Lilly and got to "I inspected it" before Lilly started flipping quickly through the pages by herself. Hen grew a bit hungry looking at the pictures as they swiftly flipped by. *Apple pie sounds good, actually. Too bad it's so time consuming…and I almost always either burn the edges or leave the center raw. Maybe we can stop by the bakery and pick one up sometime this week.*

Hen was torn from her thoughts as she heard Lilly begin to rip out a page.

"Careful, Lil. We want to take good care of our things so they can last a long time. Gentle hands with this old book, okay?" Lilly looked up with big, sad eyes.

"It's okay. No harm done. Do you want Mommy to keep reading?"

Lilly nodded.

"Okay, let's see, 'T took it'…" Mrs. Nettles' note on the page stopped Hen in her tracks.

I know what you've been doing, T, she had written in red ink.

Hen gave the book back to Lilly and thought for a moment. *T…as in Tom? Who was Tom exactly? What did he take? Maybe it was T as in Tittle.* Hen needed to know more before she started making accusations. From what she knew, pretty much everyone loved Derrick Tittle. If she learned anything from the news about Georgie, her actions had real life consequences. She definitely wasn't ready to confront anyone before she had all the evidence sorted out.

Perhaps she'd call Gene… or maybe she should go directly to the police. Hen let out a frustrated sigh. No one was going to believe her if she started accusing a local celebrity.

Without thinking, she flicked on the switch on the lamp beside her. *How was it already getting dark?* Hen decided that it was too late to talk to anyone, though she knew deep down that she was just using that as an excuse. She didn't want to talk about arrests or embezzlement or nefarious behavior of any kind. I'm fact, she didn't want to talk to anyone else over the age of one-and-a-half for at least the rest of the day, if not the next few days.

Hen went through Lilly's bedtime routine quickly and moseyed to the kitchen to fix a cup of tea. As she dunked her cinnamon tea bag into her favorite mug decorated with Lilly's purple handprint, a knock at the door startled her.

It's eight at night. Who the heck could that be? Against her better judgement, Hen opened up her front door and stood aghast. Staring straight back at her was none other than Derrick Tittle. The wide, white grin was unmistakable, although it was much less confident a smile than the one displayed on magazine covers. Hen found herself frozen in the doorway until finally Derrick broke the incredibly awkward silence.

"Good evening. Hen, isn't it? My name is Der-"

"I know," Hen cut him off.

"Oh, yes," he answered softly and continued. "Well, you're probably wondering what I'm doing here. I'm so sorry to have disturbed your evening-"

"My baby is asleep down the hall." Hen didn't recognize her own strong and icy tone. *When a strange man appears at your door at night, perhaps the inner mom-strength kicks in*, Hen thought to herself, *like those women who are on the news picking up cars to save their children.* Except instead of lifting vehicles, Hen was acting slightly off-putting to a man who already seemed incredibly uncomfortable in her presence. She still felt tough. *Almost the same.*

"I am so sorry." Derrick looked ashamed, but he never broke eye contact. Hen believed him, he really did seem to be sorry for disturbing her. Whatever ere of confidence he was used to putting on was now completely gone. Now it was her turn to break the silence.

Hen softened her tone just a little, "What are you doing here, Mr. Tittle?"

Derrick began to explain, "Well, I'm here on account of my cousin, Gene. You know Gene?"

"I do."

"Oh good." He was flustered. "Well, he told me you wished to speak with me." Hen could see him carefully choosing his words.

"So, you decided to come to my house, unannounced, after dark because Gene told you that I wanted to speak with you?"

"Oh…right. When you put it that way, um-"

"Why are you really here?" Hen's voice had regained its chilly tone.

"Um, well, I think that Gene may have accidentally given you something that belongs to me…by mistake."

"You mean the evidence of your embezzlement?" Hen heard the words tumble out of her mouth before she had the chance to think it through. It was a shot in the dark, but she knew that she had to be onto something. Derrick's face was as white as a ghost, even in the darkness of the evening.

"Wh-wh-what do you know?" he stuttered.

"I know that you should go to the police." Who was this powerful, no-nonsense woman who had taken over Hen's body?

"It's not what you think." Derrick looked away for the first time since the start of the conversation. Hen likened him to a scolded puppy, tail between his legs. Taking a deep breath, he met Hen's eyes once again. "Please, let me explain." There was something about the sincerity in his eyes.

Hen closed her eyes and begrudgingly agreed. "Okay, I'll hear you out." Derrick's face lit up. "But not tonight," Hen continued, "and not here. Let's meet at Harrison's Bakery tomorrow around noon. I'll bring the packet, but don't get any ideas about taking it. I've made a digital copy."

"Deal," Derrick eagerly agreed. "Thank you, Hen." He smiled at her as he turned and walked away.

What in the world just happened? Hen's head was spinning. She tried to look at the bright side. *At least I have a reason to get pie tomorrow.*

CHAPTER TWENTY-ONE

Hen pulled her cardigan tighter around her and shifted her weight once more on the hard metal chair. The bistro-style tables in the bakery seating area were far from comfortable. *Who was it that came up with waffle pattern metal seats anyway? Were they making breakfast using their waffle iron and thought, "You know what? That looks comfortable! Instead of cooking on it, let's sit on it instead."* Hen stood up for a moment as she slid a hardcover book from her bag beneath her. She was freezing, having occupied the table furthest from the ears of other patrons, which happened to be directly under the fan.

She glanced up at the cuckoo clock sticking out from the wall right above her head. She had been waiting on that uncomfortable little chair for ten minutes and still Derrick Tittle had not arrived. However, in his defense, she had shown up thirteen minutes early.

Hen was never early. In fact, she was usually late, except, that is, when she was particularly anxious about something. Having had an entire sleepless night to mull over the impending conversation, she found herself looking up all she could on Tittle and his organization: The Foundation of Inspiration. Unfortunately, even after several hours of late-night digging, she hadn't learned much more than what she'd originally gleaned from the local newspaper. This led to Hen filling ill-prepared and anxious for her meeting with the local celebrity.

Thus, today, she had dropped off Lilly in record time and arrived with thirteen minutes to spare. One more glance at the clock. A few more seconds and Derrick would be late.

Cuckoo! Cuckoo! Hen nearly jumped out of her seat, like a frozen waffle popping out of a toaster. She was so startled from the tolling of the clock that she hardly noticed the tall, dapper man pulling out the chair across from her.

"You alright there?" he asked, sitting down.

"Oh, Mr. Tittle. Hello. You're right on time."

"I make an effort to be prompt. Especially when I'm dealing with something that is particularly important. Also, feel free to call me Derrick." His unbroken eye contact made Hen a little wary. He was much more composed than he had been the previous evening.

You have the upper hand, Hen. Don't forget, she reminded herself.

"So, what is it that you want to talk to me about?" Hen asked, trying to match Derrick's level of confidence.

"Let's get some coffee and a scone or something and I'll start from the beginning," he suggested. "I think we go up to the counter to order. It's on me…what would you like?"

"A slice of apple pie, please, and cinnamon ice-cream."

"A cup of coffee as well?"

"Yeah, that too, a little cream and one sugar."

"Coming up."

He sauntered up to the counter as Hen stayed planted at the table, wondering how to not look awkward sitting by herself. She began fiddling with her hair, twisting it in between her fingers, but caught herself fidgeting and put her hands in her lap. She reached for her phone but didn't want to be one of those people mindlessly swiping around plastered to a tiny screen looking at nothing, so she pulled her empty hand back out of her purse. She looked up once more at the cuckoo clock. Lilly would love it. The little blue birds perching in the windows. *It looks so quaint. That is until it scares the pants off of you every hour.* Perhaps every cuckoo clock wasn't quite as obnoxiously loud, but one thing was for sure, Hen was not going to buy one to find out.

"Gorgeous, isn't it?" Derrick imparted as he placed two plates of pie and two cups of coffee on the small table. Hen looked up to see he had followed her gaze to the clock.

"Oh, yeah. Really intricate…A bit *loud* though."

Derrick laughed. "Yes, it is. I saw you jump as it rang twelve when I was walking in." Hen felt her face go pink but was relieved that Derrick didn't notice. He was fixated on the cuckoo. "You know, people say 'they just don't make them like they used to' about a number of old things, but when it comes to cuckoo clocks, they just don't make them at all anymore, very few anyway, to this detail."

Hen chimed in, "You used to fix up things like this, didn't you?"

"Still do," Derrick replied, shifting his focus back on her and taking his seat.

"Oh, I thought you did philanthropy."

"I do."

"Well, I'm confused then."

"It's more of a hobby now. I find a lot of value in what I do professionally, but there are times that I need a break. There's something about the way a clock fits together exactly right, the preciseness of it, that I find soothing." Hen nodded but kept quiet urging him continue. "There aren't single solutions to the problems of the outside world, though I wish there were. Life is messier than that. It gets complicated when you must choose between multiple resolutions. Easier to choose the wrong one. I guess what I'm saying is, when the cogs fit in multiple ways, it's easier to make a mistake."

Hen noticed Derrick's demeanor had changed. He wasn't the scared puppy of last evening, nor was he the self-assured politician that walked through the door just a moment ago. He was just a man who loved clocks.

"So, why'd you stop fixing up old clocks and things?" Hen asked once she realized Derrick was done with his last thought.

"Essie Nettles," he said definitively, locking eyes with Hen once again.

"Wait, what?"

"Yep," Derrick continued. "She said I had the 'strength of heart' for philanthropic work. She even took me under her wing a bit. Essie was very much involved in charity work of her own."

"That was really cool of her," Hen remarked.

"It was." Derrick nodded. "Until she thought she could make me do everything under the sun in the name of 'charity'. I hardly had a cent to my name and found myself completely reliant on the pittance that she offered in exchange for my help."

"Oh, really? That doesn't seem like her..." Hen blurted out. She pursed her lips tightly, immediately regretting the remark.

"You knew her too?" He sounded incredibly surprised.

"No, no. I, uh, just read about her...you know, when all that stuff was in the news about the missing fortune and everything." Hen heard her voice quicken its pace as she attempted to explain away Derrick's suspicion.

He seemed to believe her. "Well, you can't trust all that you read." He flashed a very white, wide grin at Hen and continued, "Not that she wasn't a fine lady. I don't mean it that way. She certainly taught me a great deal. I wouldn't be where I am today without her." Hen nodded and smiled, careful not to talk too much and instead be the listener, while Derrick did the talking. *Wise owl.*

He went on, "Essie and I didn't always agree though. She was very particular about *who* she helped. They needed to *deserve* her help, you see, or she felt she'd be wasting her time. I'm not sure if it was due to her ego of having been a successful actress or just her attitude of wanting to do things her own way, but when I started my own fundraising, she wanted to maintain control over everything I was doing, who I was helping, and how the funds were distributed. I had to make the difficult decision to cut ties with her. I don't know if she ever realized how guilty I felt for doing that. I went about it all wrong. I was young. I don't think she ever forgave me. I had wasted her time, you see."

"Did she ever reach out to you or you her?" Hen asked.

"Never."

Hen paused to think before she chimed back in.

"So, what exactly does this have to do with the papers from Gene?"

Derrick sighed a heavy sigh. He looked down at his hands, gulped down a long sip of coffee, then met Hen's gaze once more. "I haven't always been successful. You go through ups and downs. I was reliant on donations but didn't always raise the money that I thought I would. I had promised to help people. I started to put more and more of my own money into the fund. And when I ran out, I took money that I didn't have from those who did. It wasn't much at first, you know, but I had to get the ball rolling. I found myself worse off than some of the people I had set out to help."

He took another drink, then continued, "And then, it happened. I had my first really successful fundraiser. It was incredible. I was able to form a set salary for myself to continue doing this full-time. I began to notice that the biggest turnouts were the larger, fancier events. And so, I put on my first gala. Bought myself a tux and new shoes and wouldn't you know it, it was more profitable than I ever could have imagined. I should have just paid back what I took initially, but I was in deeper than I wanted to admit.

As I rubbed elbows with the elite, I began to realize the importance of my image. The better I looked, the more money people were willing to donate. The higher my social status, the greater the success of my philanthropy. It wasn't until I was fully immersed in this world, did I realize that I was in over my head.

So, I began to take a bit more than my allotted salary, here and there. I reasoned that it was a business expense, investing in my image to raise more for the people I would be helping. I kept track of what I took off the top with every intention to repay it myself. No one was checking my work. No one knew. It was actually incredibly easy to take a little extra. It's a lesson that I wish I'd never learned."

Derrick stopped for a moment to look out the window. He finished off his coffee and readjusted himself on the chair.

Then, seemingly gaining a second wind, he continued, "I never really discuss the work we do at Foundation of Inspiration. It's intentionally vague. You see, we don't turn people away. It's basically a means for anyone, anywhere to get back on their feet. Most especially those that have exhausted other options," Derrick explained and paused pointedly.

"That sounds great though," Hen said, noticing that he expected a response.

"It is. I believe it is. But the donors who give the large chunk of the funding don't necessarily agree. It is easy to find people who want to support a hard-working single mom with a sick kid. I'm so glad that we can be there to help families like that, but to be honest, someone else is usually willing to give support first.

Now that we are a large organization, we have the resources to search for support for those that need it. The stories like that one, they make it easy to find support elsewhere. But the alcoholic who can't seem to get his life together, his story is less attractive to potential donors. No one wants to help the people society considers bums or jerks or misanthropists. It's where so much of our money goes, though."

"But wait, what does that have to do with the money you took for yourself?" Hen found herself asking a little louder than she intended.

"Shh! I am not proud of that. I'd appreciate if you didn't shout it for everyone to hear."

"Oops, sorry," Hen whispered.

"Well, I kept track of what I had pilfered over the years, but I'm ashamed to admit, though it didn't seem to be that much at one time, years and years of taking a little bit has become a lot. It became too daunting a task. I haven't taken anything beyond my salary for a long time, however."

"Don't you feel terrible about it? Taking money that people donated and using it on yourself?"

"Yes and no. I have to make a living too, you know. It's a lesson I learned in those early days. I'm no good to anyone if I don't at least take care of myself. But yes, I do wish I wouldn't have gotten sucked into that world. It all comes back to Essie. She warned me of that very thing. On the day she died, I retrieved the paperwork that I'd kept detailing what I had taken and hid it in a box full of paperwork in Gene's office at the body shop. I always got the feeling that she was keeping tabs on me, just waiting for me to mess up somehow. She was vindictive in that way, you know. I felt so uneasy even just having the papers in my office. I hid them behind lock and key, of all things."

"You hid them? Then why give them to Gene?" Hen asked.

"He never looks at his paperwork! I figured it'd be a safe way to keep a copy that no one would ever look at. And somehow made me feel less guilty having it out of my office."

"Yeah, Gene's paperwork was kind of a mess. You know, I think he suspects that you haven't been fully honest," Hen said.

"What do you mean?" Derrick inquired.

"He mentioned something about you seeming fake, like you were acting a part rather than just being you."

Derrick sighed and said softly, "Gene really does know me well." He seemed troubled by the notion of disappointing his cousin. Hen felt a little guilty for having brought it up.

"I found a notebook and business card from your old repair business," Hen said, hoping to lighten the mood.

"Really?" Derrick's eyes lit up. "I miss those days. Do you think I could have them back?"

"Yes," Hen answered, "but, I still think you need to speak with the police about your past. It's definitely still haunting you. Maybe owning up will finally let you move on."

"I would, but I don't want scandal. If word gets out about this, any of this, the money I took, the real beneficiaries of the foundation, I could lose funding. I can't in good conscience do that just to feel better myself. People need our organization."

"But what if the whole thing could be taken care of discreetly? Wouldn't you rather come forward now than worry about someone else finding out later?"

"You've got a point." Derrick pondered on it for a moment. "What's your stake in all of this?"

Hen shrugged.

"Oh, no," Derrick retorted. "I've just given you the whole story. The least you can do is tell me why you've got such a vested interest."

He was right. He'd been completely open and honest with her. They were out of earshot of any other customers and the woman behind the counter had left the vicinity to decorate cakes in the back room. Something came over Hen. She needed to tell someone. Someone who actually knew Mrs. Nettles. Hen decided to take a gamble. She took a deep breath and opened her case file.

CHAPTER TWENTY-TWO

Derrick leaned back in his chair. "So, Essie has been harassing people from beyond the grave. That's intense even for her. And she was kind of an intense person to begin with."

"She's not really the one I'm worried about," Hen said, almost under her breath.

"What do you mean by that?" Derrick's tone immediately became more serious.

"Nothing..." Hen didn't really want to get into the mysterious note or text from the unknown caller just yet. There was still a chance, however slim, that he could be involved somehow. "What I mean is, her notes seem less antagonistic and more just like spooky puzzles. She left clues that hinted to you actually."

"Hold on, you're saying that Essie Nettles left you hints... about me?"

"Well, not exactly," Hen continued, "but in the right context, it makes a lot of sense. It was her puzzles that led me to George Nettles-Brown and all his shenanigans, you know."

"You mean to say that you were involved in unearthing The Great Golden Goose's Antiques scandal? I had no idea!"

"Well, no one does really. I dropped off the evidence anonymously. Mrs. Nettles was really the one who figured it out, though. That's what I mean. Did she know about your, um, temporarily…overly generous salary?"

"Thank you for phrasing that more graciously. And to answer your question, I don't know, though I always suspected she did. She was a bit of a busybody, especially in her later years. She hardly opened her door for anyone, and yet she knew everything that was going on, everyone's personal business. Like I said before, I felt like she was waiting for me to mess up. No wonder I felt such an imposition to get those papers out of my office…like anyone would have found them otherwise."

"Why did you hide them in the first place?"

"As you saw, I kept a clear account of the money I had taken. It was my own fastidious way of making sure I could pay it back eventually. Only eventually never came. I hid them in my office drawer and even hid the key. It cut a little hole into a book on the shelf and concealed the key inside in case I ever needed to open my locked drawer. It's a little trick I picked up from reading old detective novels as a kid. There were a few sentimental valuables inside as well."

"But what if you forgot where you hid the key?"

"That wouldn't happen. I always kept it in the fourteenth book on the fourth row of the center bookshelf." He paused a second, then continued, "I never shared that location with anyone before. Not that it matters now. I've since emptied that drawer and put my valuables in a safety deposit box."

Hen thought for a moment and began flipping through her case file. "Why do those numbers sound so familiar? Fourteen and four…" she ruminated aloud. "Here!" Hen pointed to the second drawing. It was a crude map, just like that of the antiques store bathroom complete with a tiny 'x' and 4/14 scribbled near the top.

"I can't believe it…" Derrick's voice trailed off for a moment as he focused in on the drawing. "She figured it out somehow. That is my office. This is a map of my office. How the he-"

"Hey," Hen interrupted. "It's okay. Just figure out a way to pay it back over time and come clean about it. You are in control. Not her."

"Well yeah! She's dead!" Derrick was on the border of shouting. Two elderly women with matching shades of gray-blue hair sitting a few tables away turned their heads toward their table while a large man in a fedora sitting alone clear across the room looked up from his newspaper. Derrick must have realized that he was speaking loud enough to cause a scene and immediately lowered his voice. "The thought of her *spying* on me makes me intensely uncomfortable. I mean, she was privy to my private information. It's violating."

"I get that," Hen responded honestly. After a slightly awkward silence that lasted a beat too long, she asked, "If you don't want to, that's fine, but do you think you could shed any light on any of these other clues?"

Derrick sighed. "I could try. I was never very good at those kinds of puzzles. One time, Essie gave me a puzzle box under the guise of a repair job. I never did figure it out. The smug look on her face when I returned it unopened, like she expected me to do so…" He furrowed his brow. "I should have smashed it with a hammer when I had the chance."

Hen waited for him to calm down once more then laid down a twenty on the table. "I really appreciate you being so open with me. You don't have to pay for this today. Consider this the first little bit to help you pay back what you owe to the people who really need it."

Derrick smiled his characteristic wide smile. "Okay. You win. I know a few decent guys I can talk to on the force. I'll own up to it discreetly if that's even possible."

"Good."

"But you have to come with me," he added.

Hen rolled her eyes. "Fine, but I can't stay long because I have to pick up my daughter. We've already been here longer than I had planned."

And so, Hen packed up her bag and walked out with Derrick to the parking lot. They had inadvertently parked in adjoining spaces. Hen was surprised to notice that Derrick wasn't opening the door to some shiny new sports car, just a common old four-door sedan. Though, she did take note that it was spotlessly clean.

She entered on the driver's side of her less-than-spotlessly clean minivan and followed Derrick's car to the station. She was beyond grateful that the receptionist wasn't behind the counter as they made their way in. Four or five people must have greeted Derrick from the time he set foot out of his car door to when he knocked on the door to an unmarked office at the end of the hall. Hen couldn't remember the last time she had four people go out of their way to say hello to her in a single day, let alone a single walk from the car. She felt like a groupie, and to be honest, she wasn't crazy about the comparison.

"I don't really know if you need me here," Hen whispered to Derrick as they stood outside the door.

"You're uncomfortable," he stated aloud. It was more of an observation than a question.

"Well, yeah, kind of," Hen admitted.

"Alright. I understand. Go ahead. I'll be fine."

"Thanks. And good luck."

Hen turned to leave, ready to bolt, but Derrick tapped her shoulder.

"Hen, before you go. I just want to thank you. I've needed this push for a long time. I'm going to make things right." He made the prolonged eye contact that Hen was becoming more used to. Hen smiled, nodded, and turned back around. She was halfway down the hallway when she heard the door creak open.

She didn't turn her head to see, but heard a large, deep voice bellow, "Derry! What a pleasant surprise! To what do I owe the pleasure, old friend?"

"Well, to be honest, Bill, I could use your advice. I have a lot I want to talk about. You got some time?"

"Of course! Come on in…"

The men's voices became muffled as the door closed behind them. *He'll be fine.* Hen assured herself. She was proud of herself, and of Derrick, and she couldn't help but think that Mrs. Nettles would have been a little proud of him too.

23

CHAPTER TWENTY-THREE

Living in a small-ish town had its perks. The clerk behind the meat counter at Randell's Food Mart knew Hen's order without her having to shout over the far-too-loud ambient noise of the local grocery store. *Half a pound of honey ham, half a pound of turkey, one pound of sliced American- the fancy brand because it was ten times better than the cheap cheese-like substitute and worth the extra dollar fifty.*

However, life in a town that size also had its downfalls. Cliques that started with geeks and cheerleaders in high school later morphed into knitter's club members and gym rats by adulthood. Hen wasn't really the type of person who identified with any particular group, especially now that her main companion was too young to hold knitting needles or dumbbells. If she was completely honest with herself, it was lonely at times.

She hated taking Lilly to spend the day or even a few hours at her mom's because it left her with moments like this, where she found herself walking to her car alone in the expanse of a quiet, empty parking lot, left with nothing but her thoughts.

She missed Lilly even though she'd only just dropped her off that morning. She missed Harry and hated admitting it, but she was mad at him for being gone so frequently even though she knew he was trying to do what was best. She missed Abby. Why did she have to move so far away? Why did Hen keep pushing her friend away?

She even missed hearing from Mrs. Nettles. She hadn't received anything from her since the Tom, the Piper's Son notecard.

She's not my friend. Hen reminded herself. *She's also dead. It's not even Mrs. Nettles sending me these things. It's…someone else.*

Hen stopped in her tracks and turned around to look past the police station and the community center to another small structure that shared the same parking lot. That was another benefit to living in a small-ish town. The post-office was conveniently located right next to all the other community buildings. *If anyone knew anything about mail, it would have to be a post-office worker, right?* That made sense to Hen as she pivoted and continued her stride toward the unassuming little building.

The door swung open easily as if it were made of cardboard as she entered. It was ostensibly empty, though Hen thought she heard some rummaging around from behind the counter, so she cautiously made her way further into the room.

"Hello?" Hen called out. "Anybody here?"

"Hey!" A head popped up from behind the counter in response to her call like a jack-in-the-box. Hen nearly jumped out of her skin and let out a pathetic little scream. She hated jack-in-the-boxes. Always did.

"Geez!" she said, holding her heart and catching her breath.

"Oh man. Sorry there, Hen. Didn't mean to scare you…you know, again." Hen recognized the voice. She looked up and met eyes with Thad Neilson.

"Since when do you work at the post-office?" Hen asked, now having composed herself a bit.

"For a while now, I guess. You don't come in here often I suppose." Thad answered back. He was right. She couldn't remember the last time she physically walked into the post-office. Apparently neither did anyone else. Not a soul walked in or out.

"Hey, thanks for helping me the other day," Hen said quietly. The silence of the empty room made her fight the urge to whisper.

"Oh, sure," he responded then turned and began sorting what looked like empty envelopes. Hen waited for Thad to continue the conversation, to start asking questions about the box she had him carry into the station and Hen's admittedly cryptic instructions to not look inside, but he didn't. In fact, Thad didn't say another word about it.

Maybe he simply didn't care. Hen reminded herself that she was perhaps abnormally curious and most people, particularly most men, didn't overthink things the way she did.

Hen glanced around once more and concluded that no one else would be entering the old post-office any time soon. Thad was her only option at this point in time if she wanted any answers about her mystery mailer.

"So…Thad. I was wondering if I could ask you a question."

"Shoot," Thad responded, his back to her as he grabbed a few small brown boxes out of a giant canvas bin. Hen was a bit offended that he didn't even look up at her, but also a little relieved. She had a terrible poker-face and most likely looked very uncomfortable.

"Well, if someone sent a letter to someone but didn't incl-"

"Wait." Thad stopped and turned to look at Hen quizzically. "You're asking me a question about mail?"

"Well…yeah. I mean we're in a post-office and you work here. Why is that so surprising?" Hen tried to read the look on Thad's face. She couldn't. He was probably an excellent poker player. That or he never owned a deck of cards in his life.

"You're right. It's not. Continue." He went back to his work as Hen went on.

"Okay, so, as I was saying, if someone sent a letter to someone else but didn't include their return address, is there any way to figure out who sent it?"

"Are we talking specifically a letter or a package?"

"I don't know," Hen shrugged. "Does it matter?"

"No, not really. I'd say you might be on a wild goose chase."

Hen paused for a moment. "I didn't say that it was sent to me."

Thad glanced over his shoulder at her and turned around. Then he sauntered over and leaned his elbow on the counter.

"You didn't," he said, "but you made the trip all the way here, and you're asking me about it, so, I figured."

Hen rolled her eyes and sighed, "Okay. So how do I know who sent it?"

Thad seemed to give her his full attention for the first time since she'd walked through the door. "Maybe they don't want you to find out."

Hen wasn't sure how to respond. There was an awkwardly long silence as a result.

"Or," Thad continued, "maybe it was just a scatter-brained relative who forgot to sign their name. If you are really curious, you could ask around to your family and friends. Did you try posting on social media about it?"

"No," Hen replied.

Thad shrugged then continued doing whatever he was doing with the bin full of boxes, "Hmm, well, that's all the advice I have."

Something felt off about Thad. Why did he keep turning away from her? Why had he seemed so skeptically uninterested? Hen assumed she came off as suspicious, especially since handing him the box of evidence to take into the police station. She wanted one more look at him face-to-face.

Hen walked up to the counter, "Oh, hey Thad? Could I also get a sheet of stamps?" He grabbed two sheets and met her eyes from behind the counter.

"Coffee cups or phases of the moon?" he asked, holding one up at a time.

"Definitely the coffee," Hen answered and watched him closely as he rung her up. She couldn't get anything from his expression. *He really should think about playing poker.*

She paid and said a polite goodbye, tucking the stamps into her purse and leaving the post-office. Returning to her car, Hen looked back one more time at the small building behind her and noticed a tiny window that looked out onto the parking lot. Thad was standing directly in front of the window, but not looking at her, though he soon met her gaze and gave a friendly wave.

Hen waved back awkwardly and made her way to the car. She threw her purse on the passenger's seat and clicked her seatbelt. *So, that interaction with Thad was weirder than normal, right?* Or, maybe she was over-thinking things.

Hen made the drive out to her mom's and offered to order some pizza since she had taken so long to get back. She was happy to just let her mom talk. Topics included but were not limited to: the rising cost of dry-cleaning, the neighbor who adopted a sixth cat, the packing list for her upcoming trip, the benefit to always salting your pasta water, and that one handsome actor whose name she forgot from that one movie whose title she couldn't remember.

Hen smiled, nodded, listened, and chowed down on her pepperoni, grateful to have her daughter on her lap and a reprieve from having to talk herself. After a few hours of a very long, mostly-one-sided conversation, Hen and Lilly packed up and headed home.

On the drive home, Hen said to her daughter in the back, "You know what, Lilly? After that whole time, I can't remember a single thing that Grandma was telling me about." Hen laughed at herself. Guess Hen wasn't as curious a person as she thought herself to be. "What do you remember?"

"Pizza!" Lilly jeered. Hen laughed harder than she probably should have. *Yep, same here, kiddo.*

Hen, with Lilly on her hip, made her way to the porch and flung the door open, just as she did every other time they came home. This time, however, she didn't walk into a quaint living room with a few toys tossed about. The sight before her took Hen's breath away.

Her house, her beautiful little home, had been ransacked. Couches and furniture turned over, broken glass on the floor from a smashed first floor window, what she assumed was the point of break-in. A terrifying thought came into Hen's mind. She didn't know if whoever it was that had broken into her house and made this mess had actually left. Perhaps they were still there. Nothing inside was important enough for her to risk finding out, and before she took another step, Hen held on extra tight to Lilly and ran back to her car, locking the doors and calling 9-1-1.

CHAPTER TWENTY-FOUR

The next few hours were a blur. Police lights, answering countless questions from officers, a million thoughts running through Hen's mind without any time or wherewithal to process a single one of them. She felt her body shaking from sheer adrenaline as she held tightly to her precious baby. Lilly's head felt heavy on her shoulder and her legs dangled below. She was completely exhausted, and thankfully, completely unaware of the severity and fearfulness of what was happening.

Whoever it was that had broken in had fled before the police inspected the house. Even though they gave Hen the go-ahead to look around and see if she noticed if anything of value was missing, assuring her that it was safe, she still found herself taking shallow breaths and tiptoeing about as if to not to disturb the crime scene. And that's what it was: a crime scene. Her own home suddenly seemed so unfamiliar to her.

She had checked every room except one, the nursery. Hen took a deep breath and opened Lilly's door to great relief. It looked exactly as she had left it. Drawers closed, rocking chair positioned upright, Lilly's dollies all sitting happily upon their shelf. All at once, a wave of emotion washed over her, and Hen found herself weeping uncontrollably on the little pink rug in the center of Lilly's room.

Lilly, who had started to wake at the sight of her own room, toddled over to her stuffed animals and began playing. Hen, however, remained a puddle in the middle of the room. A police officer stood uncomfortably in the doorway, unsure of how to respond to the despondent woman before him.

"So, uh, ma'am. We've boarded up that window for you," the officer voiced kindly. Hen knew he was trying to be helpful, but she was too much a wreck to carry on a normal conversation.

"We are going to need to head out here, ma'am. Are you going to be alright?" Hen continued sobbing, unable to compose herself enough to answer.

"She's pretty tough, officer. She'll be okay," Hen heard a wonderfully familiar voice respond.

She immediately stopped crying into her hands and spun around. Hen could hardly believe it. There, standing in the doorway of the nursery, was Abby. Hen couldn't think of a time that she needed her best friend more than at this very moment.

She jumped up and ran over to her, Abby throwing her arms around her friend.

"It's going to be okay," Abby whispered into Hen's ear.

The officer nodded and said something about contacting the station if they noticed anything else of consequence or needed any further assistance. In all honesty, Hen wasn't really paying attention as well as she should have to his exact remarks before he left and made his way out. All she knew was that she wasn't alone. Abby was there. It was going to be okay.

After the hug that lasted an eternity, Hen followed her normal night routine with Lilly and tiptoed back through the house to meet Abby in the kitchen.

"Tea?" Abby offered, holding out a steaming mug. Hen nodded and turned the kitchen stools back around the right way so that she could sit down. For a long time, the women sat in silence.

Finally, Hen spoke up, "What...what are you doing here?" Her throat was sore from sobbing and her voice was weak.

"I was worried about you," Abby answered straightforwardly. "I'm sorry I upset you, Hen. Sometimes I say things and they don't come out the way I mean them to. Can I tell you something?"

Hen nodded as she sipped her tea.

"I think you are amazing." Hen blinked back at her. She felt like she had been such a lousy friend to Abby. She didn't deserve the compliment. Perhaps Abby was just being nice because she felt sorry for her. Her friend continued, "I mean, you're a great mom. You're a supportive wife. You are smart and caring and patient." She paused and waited until Hen made eye contact with her. "But you never ask for anything, Hen. You never expect anything from anyone." Abby had said that last sentence like she was pointing out a flaw. Hen thought about that for a minute. She had always prided herself on her self-sufficiency.

Abby went on, "I've known you since grade school, Henny, and for the longest time, I was unaware of when you needed help because you never let it show. But I know you pretty well now and I can tell when things aren't right." Abby was noticeably worried. "A lot has been going on in your life lately and you've been taking care of things all on your own. I guess what I'm saying is that you don't have to anymore."

Hen's shoulders relaxed. She grabbed for Abby's hand and squeezed, "Okay," Hen said softly. Even though it was one single word, they both knew the weight carried within that 'okay'. *Okay, I forgive you for the grudge I've been holding. Okay, I appreciate you coming here more than words can express. Okay, I'm ready to be fully honest about all that's going on. Okay, I really do need you.*

"Okay, then." Abby flashed a genuine smile at her best friend. "Let's put your house back together." She glanced around, "You know, you've really let this place go. Did you throw a raging party last night or what?"

Hen laughed. "Yeah, you know me."

Abby gave her hand one more squeeze back and with true sincerity whispered, "Yeah, I do."

The two women tidied up what they could, and Abby pulled out the sleeping bags while Hen ran the vacuum a final time. They were setting up a sleepover in the hall outside of Lilly's nursery. Hen knew it was the only way she would be able to make it through the night.

That didn't mean that she would be able to sleep, however. Abby graciously agreed to stay up all night if Hen wanted which led to the decision to have an old-fashioned sleepover. They lit a few jar candles, chatted about old times, painted their toenails, and ate whatever junk food was left from the back of the kitchen cabinet, hugging their pillows and sitting on sleeping bags in their pajamas like teenagers.

"For a while there, I was really enjoying the whole mystery of it. It was like a fun puzzle figuring out the clues hidden in the books and nursery rhymes," Hen found herself explaining, "until I got this note. It seemed almost threatening. Someone knew everything that had gone on with Georgie and they let me know about it."

"Whoa, that's creepy. What did it say?" Abby was laying on her stomach, hands propping up her chin, wide-eyed in anticipation.

"I kept the note in this bag I've been carrying around with me. I think in the flurry of everything that I dropped it by the front door. I'll grab it." Hen retrieved the bag as quickly and quietly as she could with the unusual feeling of being afraid in her own house. She plopped it on the ground, and it landed with a thump. Both women held their breath, waiting for a cry from Lilly from the other side of her door. Hen glanced at the baby monitor thankful to see her baby sleeping soundly.

"Oops," Hen whispered.

Abby smiled and turned her attention to the contents of the bag sitting before her. "Ooh! Is this the case file you've been assembling? This is full of stuff, Henny! You've become quite the detective."

"Hardly!" Hen laughed. "I've mostly just been copying down Mrs. Nettles' notes. It's like those books she sent me were full of secrets, almost like a diary. She even had these little hand-drawn maps. Only, I didn't figure out where they were about until after the fact. They are kind of cryptic"

"Whoa! Really? Where were they about?"

"One was the bathroom at the antiques shop, pointing out where to find that creepy camera. And when I met with Derrick Tittle, he said that the second one was a drawing of his office and where to find those incriminating documents."

"That's crazy." Abby rolled onto her back holding Hen's case file in her hands. "There's a third one too! Where's this one from?"

Hen shrugged, "I don't know."

"Yet!" Abby swiftly sat up. "You should keep that paper with you, Hen. You never know, you might recognize it somewhere."

Hen shrugged once more, "Maybe. It's just a bunch of boxes though. Honestly, I think you're giving me too much credit. Most of what I've written down was straight from those books she sent. And a lot of what I've figured out was kind of by accident."

Abby was flipping through each page of Hen's notes with deliberation. "Geez, this woman loved nursery rhymes."

"You're telling me. She even used nursery rhyme stationery," Hen replied.

"Wait, really?"

"See for yourself. Here's the cards she sent."

"That is really weird, now that I think about it. Not just these slightly disturbing illustrations, but the fact that you've heard from her this many times," Abby replied.

"Why do you say that?" Hen asked.

"Well, because she's dead, Henny. I mean, at least we think she's dead. How could she send you all these?"

"I don't know," Hen answered, honestly. "I actually stopped by the post-office to ask about how to find out the identity of an anonymous sender. Thad works there now. He was less than helpful."

Abby rolled her eyes, "Ugh, what did you expect from Thad?"

"Yeah, he said I was on a wild goose chase."

Abby smiled, "A wild *Mother Goose* chase!"

Hen chuckled, "Right."

"Also, I think he's wrong," Abby said. "I'm pretty sure there is a way to figure out where a piece of mail came from. Do you still have the boxes from all the books that were sent to you?"

Hen sighed, "No, I threw them out a while back. But they were just plain cardboard boxes. There wasn't anything written on them."

"Well, maybe there's something on or in the books themselves? Where are they?"

"I doubt it. I've read through them cover to cover. You're welcome to take a look for yourself." Hen said. "They are in the spare room."

Abby creaked open the door and tiptoed into the room, flicking on the light. There was a prolonged pause filled with sounds of Abby rustling about until she finally reemerged in the hallway.

"Henny, they're not here."

Hen's heart began to pound in her chest. It all made sense now. That's why the burglar didn't make it to Lilly's room at the end of the hall. They had already found what they were looking for: Mrs. Nettles' books. Whatever secrets had been hidden inside them, someone went through a heck of a lot of trouble to get them back.

CHAPTER TWENTY-FIVE

Mrs. Nettles' puzzles had become real. What's more, real danger had made its way into Hen's home. She had never been one to be driven by malintent, but that changed the moment she realized that this mysterious stranger was willing to purloin her family's safety. She needed to get to the bottom of this as soon as possible.

After whipping up some waffles for a brain-food breakfast, Hen, Abby, and Lilly set to work in the kitchen: Hen scouring through her case file and Mrs. Nettles' books and notes that remained stashed in her bag, Abby searching every corner of the internet on Hen's computer for some bit of information that would lead them in the right direction, and Lilly banging a wooden spoon on every pot, pan, and bowl that Hen could drag out of the cupboard as a means to entertain her.

For a while, Lilly seemed to be the only one making progress. She was really going at it with the spoon on Hen's big spaghetti pot.

"Ugh. There's just so many of these nursery rhymes that she circled or underlined bits of. It's hard to know what's important and what's not," Hen lamented.

"Maybe just assume that they're all important," Abby suggested. Hen sighed since that didn't really help to narrow things down.

She flipped the page and traced along her own handwriting as she read the following poem aloud:

Eeper Weeper, chimney sweeper,

Had a wife but couldn't keep her.

Had another, didn't love her,

Up the chimney he did shove ~~her~~.

"Whoa, that's a gruesome one," Abby responded and looked up from the computer to meet eyes with Hen. "Maybe the old lady really was murdered."

"But her husband died a long time ago, so that doesn't really make sense."

"Hmm, did she write anything on it?" Abby inquired.

"The last word was crossed off and another word was written in. I think it said, 'nem'. At least that's what I wrote down here."

"'Nem?' That doesn't make sense."

"Yeah, I know," Hen said.

She turned the page to the next transcribed poem and read:

One, two, buckle my shoe

Three, four, knock at the door

Five, six, pick up sticks

Seven, eight, lay them straight

Nine, ten, a big fat hen

Eleven, twelve, dig and delve

Thirteen, fourteen, maids a-courting

Fifteen, sixteen, maids in the kitchen

Seventeen, eighteen, maids in waiting

Nineteen, twenty, my plate's empty

"I remember that one!" Abby chimed in, "Except, I always stopped at ten. 'Nine, Ten, Over again', something like that. What did she write about that one?"

"I think she just circled it. I don't know, Abs. Are we trying to make sense of the ramblings of a person who had already lost their mind?"

Abby, without missing a beat, replied, "Well, she has been right about a lot so far. I'd give her some credit."

Hen nodded. *Abby's got a point.*

She turned the page once more. She had written a giant number three at the top. Below were the titles that Mrs. Nettles had indicated, circling the number three in each of them. The list included: "Three Blind Mice", "The Three Little Pigs", and "Rub-a-Dub-Dub (Three Men in a Tub)". When Hen shared this information with Abby, she nearly jumped out of her chair.

"That's it, Henny! There's three!" Abby shouted.

"Three what?" Hen asked, glancing back down at the paper to see if she'd missed something.

"Three different parts, three different secrets, three different...people! You've already figured out the first two because you're so gosh-darn clever. One more to go!" Abby cheered.

"You really think that's what she means?" Hen asked, not quite convinced.

"I do! It makes sense, doesn't it?"

"I, uh, I guess so. I don't know, it's kind of ambiguous…" Hen responded, though Abby was on a tangent now, too excited to notice that Hen wasn't all on board with her theory.

"And I think it's a *man,*" Abby continued. "I mean, all those stories are about men, or at least male characters. Henny, we merely need to figure out who the third pig is!"

Hen paused to process this concept. She reached across the table and held in her hand the second card she had received from Mrs. Nettles, the one that had informed Hen that she had been murdered and asked her to 'bring forth justice'. The front cover art on the card was the three little pigs. *Perhaps Abby had a point.*

She held the card to show Abby its cover, at which point her friend shrieked in excitement.

"Okay then!" Abby had her get-things-done voice on. "Now we only need to figure out who the last guy is." She hesitated, "And, uh, what he did, I guess."

"Well, he broke into my house, and he murdered Mrs. Nettles," Hen retorted.

Abby considered this and asked softly, "Are you alright, Henny? We can stop if you want."

"No. I'm not alright. And no. I don't want to stop," Hen answered authoritatively.

Abby smiled. "Then let's do this."

At that moment, Lilly reached up and snatched a waffle from Abby's plate, then ran out of the kitchen giggling. Abby burst out laughing while Hen chased the cute little thief as she made her way through the house, getting syrup everywhere. "Lilly, you can't just steal waffles," she said as she ran through the hall. "Please share!"

Eventually, Hen did catch up with Lilly but not until she had nibbled half the waffle leaving a sticky trail of syrup behind her. After the mess was cleaned up, the girls reconvened in the kitchen. Abby and Hen continued researching in silence for a while, stopping only to read to Lilly and put her down for an early nap.

"She really was something, huh?" Abby said, looking at a picture of Essie Nettles in a gilded twenties-era flapper costume. Hen pulled out a chair beside her friend's and sat down to examine the photo on the laptop screen.

"Yeah, definitely meant for the stage."

"I hear she was quite the infamous starlet in her day," Abby explained. "There's this quote from her manager in this article that I read about how he was always following her around, cleaning up after her. He said she was like the glitter that adorned her many costumes, eye-catching at first but leaving behind a mess everywhere she went that he could never seem to fully clean up. Ha! A little harsh, but also kind of hilarious."

Hen chuckled, "Gee, he didn't seem to like her very much."

"I think they truly were friends, but maybe his attitude was a result of them being together all the time. He probably just got sick of her sometimes." Abby grinned at Hen, "At least I live far enough away for you to miss me every so often. It keeps you from getting sick of me." Hen wondered if Abby knew quite what an understatement that was.

"I could never get sick of you," Hen said back. "I kind of had the idea that Mrs. Nettles was a loner, though. She was always photographed by herself, and she became a sort of recluse in her final years."

"I think she stole the spotlight of basically every photo she's in, but this manager guy is in the background of a lot of these pictures. More than her own husband. Here he is again." Abby pointed to a man in the background of the photo who was wearing a zoot suit and a striped hat.

It was blurry, but something seemed so familiar about his face. Hen requested that Abby pull up another picture of him.

"Um, here. Carlston (Cats) Vericcio. He's actually *in* this one. They are at a stage premiere. It seems like he was usually pretty camera shy."

Hen grabbed Abby's arm, hard. She stared at the large man in the photograph, wearing a plain fedora and grimacing at the photographer behind the lens.

He was more than familiar to Hen. His face also brought back a flood of memories to her mind.

He was the patron at the bakery who had been reading the newspaper, the man at the grocery store that she nearly rolled over with her cart, the man who had peered at her from under his hat in the antiques shop, the judgmental man who had condemned her with his displeased gaze from behind the old computer monitor that fateful day she and Lilly had stepped through the door of the library and met Mrs. Nettles.

Abby fell completely silent, her eyes locked on Hen's face. She gently pulled her arm free from Hen's tight grasp.

"Oh my god, Henny. You know him, don't you?"

26

CHAPTER TWENTY-SIX

"I say you just get in touch with him and tell him everything that you've been involved with. Just be honest. He might be surprisingly understanding. I think it's better coming from you," Abby pleaded, following Hen around the house as she did one last quick tidy-up, double checking to make sure she had everything before she left the house.

Hen stopped and met eyes with her friend, "I promise I'll tell Harry when he gets back, okay? He's got a lot going on. There's no sense in worrying him when there's nothing he can do."

"Okay, okay. But I don't know why you have to go to Nettles Mansion after nightfall. It seems more dangerous."

"The mystery person, who may or may not be Cats Vericcio, was peering from the window last time I was there in the daytime. I swear I saw a shadow watching me. If he is spending his days there, perhaps he is going home during the evenings. I believe I have a better chance of getting in."

"So, you're still sure that the best course of action to contend with someone breaking into your house is to…break into someone's house?"

"Yes," Hen answered, point-blank.

"Okay, well, I still wish I could go with you."

"Honestly, Abs, with my mom away on her trip, I'm really relieved to be able to leave Lilly with someone I trust will keep her safe."

Abby paused and smiled, then said assuredly, "I love this little girl with everything I am."

"I know," said Hen, "me too." Then, she picked up her daughter and gave her an extra tight squeeze. "Don't worry, Tammy is meeting me there, remember? I gave you her number, so you can get in touch with her too if it makes you feel better." She handed Lilly to Abby and turned to go.

Abby grabbed her shoulder. "Just be careful, okay…and wait for this Tammy girl to get there before you go inside so you're not alone…and keep in touch with me, I'll have my phone on me at all times…and if you feel like you're in any danger, don't hesitate-"

"I'll be fine, *Mom.*" Hen interrupted. She rolled her eyes at her friend but was inwardly thankful for someone who cared enough to worry about her. With that, she hugged Abby and shut the door behind her. Hen was on her way for the third time to Nettles Mansion. But this time around, she was determined to get answers.

As she set off on the now-vaguely-familiar-drive, she began forming another list in her head. Hen would meet Tammy outside the mansion. While one of them knocked on the front door, the other would search for an alternate way in. The building was supposed to be abandoned, but Hen was now pretty confident that it was not. She hoped that she was right in supposing that whomever was inhabiting the place was only doing so by day. Either way, Hen had packed a can of pepper-spray in her purse in case something would go awry, but she prayed she wouldn't need to use it.

The sky shone pinky-orange and its reflection glittered on the damp road before her. It would be quite a beautiful night were she not filled with nerves about entering a potentially hazardous place.

It's only an old building, Hen, she assured herself. *Just old stones and bricks covered in old ivy filled with old things.* She pondered

158

on that for a moment, *Aw, shoot. It's probably full of cobwebs in there.*

As the orange hues turned to maroon and then deep purple, Hen neared closer and closer to her destination. This time, she made her way in total silence. No kiddie songs, no radio, just the rumble of the minivan's tires and the sound of her own quickening heartbeat. She was half-expecting to get another flat tire or encounter another deer, but the drive was unremarkable.

That is, until she reached the turn before the Nettles driveway. A beat-up, old, blue sedan was stopped on the side of the road. *Is this Tammy's car? Shoot, we really should have talked about what kind of car she was driving here. All I know is that she said she was borrowing her aunt's car. Does this car look like it could belong to Tammy's aunt? I wish I knew anything about Tammy's aunt.* Hen's headlights were shining on the vehicle. She decided that she couldn't determine whose car it was, but there was nothing to keep her from believing that it was, in fact, Tammy's aunt's car, so that's what she would assume for the time being.

Tammy, however, was nowhere to be found.

Hen put down her window and whisper-shouted, "Tammy! You there?" She waited. Nothing. Hen tried again a little louder this time, "Hey! Tammy! Can you hear me?" Still nothing. Hen's soft voice seemed deafening in the quietness of the night.

Okay, Hen, be smart. Just give her a call. She put her car in park and put on her four-way flashers. She wasn't sure that it was really necessary to do so, but it seemed like something she learned about when she took her driver's license test a million years ago. Hen rang Tammy and waited. As the phone rang, she saw a small light appear within the parked car. It *must* be Tammy's car after all. A phone was inside, going off. But, where was Tammy?

Hen left her car running with the headlights on in order to shed some light in the otherwise dark night. She then got out to quietly investigate. Hen tried opening Tammy's driver's side door, but it was locked. In fact, all the doors were locked. The only thing she could see inside was a large, empty drink cup and a cell phone thrown onto the passenger's seat.

Hen's nerves grew as she walked around in the dark forest, outside the protection of her car. *Perhaps Tammy already made her way to the mansion. Maybe she had car trouble and locked her phone in the car by mistake, so she couldn't call to tell me.* Hen's theory was enough justification to persuade her to get back in her minivan and head to the mansion.

She drove slowly up the long driveway and found herself in the only vehicle parked outside a very imposing edifice. The mansion itself took on an eerie quality at night. Its romantic and timeworn beauty in the daylight had been tainted by obscurity. Hen closed her eyes and took a deep breath for courage, then stepped out of her vehicle, making sure her phone was in her pocket. She couldn't risk forgetting it, especially if Tammy was without her phone.

"Made it here," she typed in a text to Abby quickly before shoving her phone into her back pocket.

Hen tiptoed around the grounds as she had around her house after the break in. She checked out the front gardens, probably once gorgeous with rose blossoms but now consumed by weeds. Slowly but surely, Hen made her way to a set of stairs that led up to the mansion and large curved door. She placed her hand on the worn wood and to her utter surprise, the door creaked open.

Tammy! She's already here. She must have let herself in and left the door ajar for me, Hen surmised. *She just can't stick to the plan, can she? It's just like when she stole everything from Georgie's office. Although...I guess that kind of worked out.*

160

Hen walked warily into the dimly lit entryway calling out, "Hello? Anyone here?" She didn't really want an answer but felt like she should ask. Somehow, that made what she was doing seem less like breaking and entering.

Hen called out once more, but this time in a whisper, "Hey! Tammy! Where are you?"

Hen felt her breath becoming shallow and rapid. *Calm down,* she tried to assure herself, *Tammy has got to be in here somewhere.* She saw a lighted room down the hallway and slowly made her way towards it. Very carefully, Hen peered in the crack of the open door into an empty room.

She nudged the door open gently and was overwhelmed by the thick odor of cigar smoke. It was an office, or maybe one would call it a study in these old fancy houses. Amazingly, not an inch of wall space was left undecorated. Shelves filled with knick-knacks and large portraits of…there she was. Essie Nettles herself.

The room Hen was standing in must have been *her* study at one time. Hen quickly spotted what she assumed was once Mrs. Nettles' desk. In the far corner of the room sat an ornate marble-top desk and on top of it, her eyes darted to something familiar: the stack of books that once sat in Hen's very own spare room.

CHAPTER TWENTY-SEVEN

Hen couldn't control her own curiosity. She walked to the corner of the room to examine the desk and its contents more closely. As she surveyed the late Mrs. Nettles' personal items cluttering the surface, she felt an eerie sense of connection with the deceased woman. Hen noticed a notepad of ivy-bordered stationery sitting neatly beside a desk set complete with all colors of pencils and pens, including blue, red, and black. The uppermost piece of stationery had been ripped off leaving only the top portion of the border. Hen was confident it was an exact match for the note she had received with the top border missing.

She noticed an extravagant-looking, velvet upholstered chair. Hen could picture Mrs. Nettles choosing such an ostentatious piece of furniture for something as mundane as a desk chair. When Hen pushed it out from under the desk, a piece of fabric that had been draped over the arm fell to the floor. After leaning down to pick it up, she held in her hand what she now recognized as a piece of silk up to the light.

Upon further examination, it wasn't just any piece of silk. It was, in fact, the turquoise scarf she had tried to purchase at the antiques shop. That seemed so long ago now, yet she recognized the unique pattern of greens and blues right away. Now that she was scrutinizing the fabric, Hen observed that the paisleys almost looked like arrows. Hen still didn't fathom why it would cost upwards of seven hundred dollars.

Something is important about this little scarf. Hen couldn't possibly leave it on the floor. She folded the thin fabric into a tiny square, small enough to slide into her pocket.

It's fine...It's not like I'm stealing a valuable antique or anything, Hen attempted to reassure herself. *Gosh, Tammy's a bad influence on me. Come to think of it, where is she?*

Hen peered around from behind the desk but couldn't see much past the yellow glow of the lamp beside her, the only source of light in the room. She began to make her way around the bulky desk when the stack of books caught her attention again. *It's crazy to think of the calamity caused by a bunch of books full of nursery rhymes.*

She quickly glanced over the cover of each, trying to see if anything came back to her. One of the books laid open on the adjacent table. The poem was one she had read before:

Lucy Locket lost her pocket,

Kitty Fisher found it;

Not a penny was there in it,

Only ribbon round it.

Beneath was scribbled a bit of Mrs. Nettles' cheeky dark witticism:

Sorry, Kitty. Go kill another old bird.

Hen's mind was racing. *Kitty... Kitty...like kitty-cat. Oh my gosh, Cats! Her manager Cats...What's-his-name...could he really have killed someone? Or maybe Mrs. Nettles had only harbored suspicions of murder.* Hen's heart was racing as she grabbed a handful of books and pushed the velvet chair out far enough to hide underneath the desk to read them discreetly. Using her phone as a flashlight, Hen discovered about a dozen missed texts from Abby. *Geez, Abs, I'm in the middle of something here.* Hen tried to quickly reassure her friend, but having no service, decided that she'd just continue with the task at hand to try and find some answers in these books and then get out of there as soon as she could.

Hen tapped on the flashlight app on her phone again and scoured page after page. Nearly every cat-related poem was marked up in some way with blue ink. Cats Vericcio *(THAT'S his name!)* was most certainly involved in some unscrupulous activity, and all clues were leading to murder. Hen shivered at the thought. No wonder he didn't want these books in anyone else's hands.

After flipping through nearly three full volumes, Hen came to what she considered one of the creepier poems, Eeper Weeper. Even in the dim glow of a cell phone flashlight, she observed that she had been wrong about the notation marked on the page. It was not "nem" but "him". This changed the last word of the poem from her to him, which now read:

Up the chimney he did shove <u>him</u>.

So, Mrs. Nettles wasn't trying to prove that Cats had killed *her*, but rather that he had killed *a man*. But which man? And had he really shoved him up a chimney? How incredibly gruesome. How was that not a headline news story that Hen or Abby had come across? Unless…no one ever found out. No one, that is, except Mrs. Nettles, and now, perhaps, Hen.

Sliding her phone back in her pocket, she snuck out from under the desk. Hen was brushing the dirt off her pants when she heard what sounded like footsteps and then the latch of the study door as it closed. Literally scared stiff, Hen remained completely still, then she quietly crept back under the desk, hiding fearfully from the stranger.

She waited for what seemed like forever. The silence was at the same time comforting and suffocating, but she stayed patient, her ears straining for any indication of a sound. And after a very, very long time, she concluded that it was safe, or, maybe she should say, as safe as it was going to be. However, by this point, Hen was spooked. She was ready to get out of there.

She tried to control her breathing. Hyperventilating wasn't going to help in this situation. She needed to get to the car, call Abby, and then worry about finding Tammy. She at least gleaned some information from her crazy break-in and could work through the details in the safety of her own house.

Hen stood up slowly, placed the books exactly where she had found them, and made her way over to the door. Her heart felt like it was about to leap out of her chest. She gently pressed her ear to the door, but still heard nothing. Hen tried to psych herself up. *Just open the door, it's now or never.* She clutched the doorknob and yanked. It didn't budge. She tried again, and again, and again to no avail. The door had been locked with her trapped inside. *Oh my gosh, I guess it's never!*

Hen's breathing was even more rapid than before. What was she supposed to do now? She had a little girl at home that needed her. Tears filled her eyes as she pulled out her phone to find it still had no service.

She closed her eyes and tried to focus. *Okay, come up with an idea. Literally anything.* She thought for a moment. Maybe she would find a secret door like in the movies. All she needed to do was locate the book that opened the secret passage. *Okay, that's stupid, next.* Maybe she could jimmy the lock. *Better idea.*

It was an old door with a considerable gap between it and the doorjamb. She had no idea how, but perhaps if she shoved something into the space, she could force the door open somehow. That was the best option she had right now.

Hen reached for a letter opener that she remembered seeing on the desk. Shoving it into the gap, she tried to manipulate it back and forth, but didn't have much luck as she had never sought to break open a door before. After a particularly vigorous attempt, she pulled out a completely bent and utterly useless piece of metal.

She needed something stronger. Hen looked frantically around. The fire poker! Perhaps she could break the door off its hinges. She wasn't particularly strong, but she was pumping with adrenaline, so it just might work. Hen went to snatch the poker, but to her surprise, it didn't lift off the base. In fact, it was attached completely. It wasn't a real poker but rather a disguised lever.

With a heavy pull, Hen manipulated the poker-lever to its downward position and watched in amazement as a tall bookshelf opened from the wall revealing the entryway to a secret passage. *What do you know? Not so stupid after all.* Hen tapped her flashlight back on and before she had time to talk herself out of it, she was through the passage and down into a deep stone staircase.

CHAPTER TWENTY-EIGHT

The passage was narrow, so much so that her shoulders nearly touched the stone walls on either side. Hen tried not to think of what vermin most likely inhabited such a dank, dark place. *But if I do see a rat, I cannot scream,* she reminded herself.

As she crept deeper and deeper down the seemingly endless staircase, she felt the temperature drop drastically. The air was wet and smelled of…well, she would rather not make the comparison to what scent was filling her nostrils, but it certainly was not pleasant. Everything seemed to be a shade of greenish gray. Even with the illumination of her cellphone flashlight, Hen struggled to distinguish exactly what she was looking at.

She nearly stumbled as she treaded out onto a hard floor after the final step. The beam of light from her phone quivered as her hands shook fearfully. Hen did her best to hold it still while she moved the light around the room. She found herself in a mostly barren cellar. Hen panned the area to take in more of her surroundings. All she could see were a few empty crates stacked beside her and the gray stone walls which curved sharply to the right, inhibiting her view of what lay before her. Every surface seemed to be dripping with what she hoped was condensation from the humid air.

There was only one way to go, so she wandered carefully forward. The passage was long, cold, quiet, and wet, and with each step, Hen felt her heartbeat grow louder in her chest. She tried not to let her mind wander to her loved ones at home. Shaking her head to clear the thought from her mind as she turned a corner and a small room appeared before her. It seemed to be a once well-used workshop of some kind. An organized pegboard on the wall contained small tools and trappings for a hobby-man. Hen pushed aside a large wrench and revealed it's shadow, formed in dust from where it was hanging. *It's been a while since anyone has been down here,* Hen surmised.

She crept gingerly about, trying to make sense of her environment without disturbing anything. Unfortunately, she almost immediately got her foot caught in a large pile of thick, tangled rope and landed on the hard floor with a thud. *Ouch!* she thought but managed to keep quiet. Brushing herself off, Hen made her way around a small metal filing cabinet. She tried to open the top drawer, however it let out a loud squeak at the very slightest tug, so she deemed it not worth her curiosity to find out what was inside. *Probably nothing,* Hen rationalized.

In the darkest corner of the room lay a pile of books which piqued her interest. *More clue-filled nursery rhymes?* Hen leaned down and picked up the stack of books, moving away from the dripping walls so that she could better examine them. However, it didn't take long for her to notice a reasonably-sized nibble on the edge of the top book's cover. She held her breath and moved the books away from her body, tilting them slightly. A handful of black droppings fell to the floor.

"Uck!" she said hastily aloud. *Get ahold of yourself, Hen. It's just mouse poop. You clean up baby poop about a million times a day. Just chill out.*

She breathed out slowly and placed the books down exactly where she was standing. Then, with her toe, she pushed them around to reveal the titles on their covers. *All old manuals! Geez, all that for nothing. Stupid rats.* At least she hadn't seen an actual rat, only the residue, but she wasn't about to continue standing in that corner until it poked its ugly head out.

Quickly, Hen scootched away from the damp corner and found herself further into the center of the room. To her left, she saw a long, dirty table. Small rusty tools and wood scraps lay upon the workbench, all of which were coated densely with dust. As Hen made her way closer, she noticed that there was a small circular object that stood out against the filthy surface. It was the only object to not be dust-covered.

Hen cautiously picked it up and examined it closely. She held in her hand what looked to be a metal button, very distinctly shaped with tiny notches all around it. In the center, she could just make out the letter 'F' fancifully engraved. Handling the button breifly left Hen's fingers covered in black filth. Upon closer examination, it was actually soot, as if the button had been pulled out of a fire.

Hen dropped it suddenly, remembering the poem she had read earlier upstairs in the study. Perhaps this button had belonged to the man to which it was referring. "Shoved up a chimney" or something, it had said. After further consideration, Hen snatched the button back up and slipped it into her pocket in case she needed to reference it later. She feverishly wiped her hands on off on her shirt. Enough investigating, she needed to get out of there.

She made her way through the room and was elated to see a small door, almost hidden by its camouflaged green-gray appearance. *Please open,* she pleaded in her head. Hen shut her eyes and tugged as hard as she could. Sure enough, the door swung open without difficultly. In doing so, Hen had been a bit overzealous causing her to fall backwards and bang loudly into a large, metal machine. After a brief examination, the machine seemed to be an old incinerator of some kind.

She made her way past the machine and through the now-open doorway. Another staircase lay before her leading up to what Hen had to assume was the main level. This time, she didn't tread lightly, in fact, she ran as fast as she could. In her haste, she slipped once, banging her knee off of one of the stone steps. Hen winced but bit her lip sharply to keep from crying out in pain. She could see a light at the top of the stairs, a straight and skinny beam of soft light…moonlight. This staircase led to an outside entrance to the cellar. Two pieces of heavy wood lay between her and a means of escape with that tiny glow of moonlight pouring coquettishly through the gap between them.

Please open. Please, she pleaded once more. But these doors were less obedient than the first. She pushed upward on the wood with all her might, but the doors had been locked from above. She pushed again, using all the strength she could muster. Still nothing.

Her arms and shoulders ached from using herself as a battering ram while her knee continued to throb. *Once more, you can do this, Hen.* With all she had, Hen pushed open the outside doors to the cellar. For a split second, she was relieved, but then, she quickly realized that they had opened way too easily, almost on their own.

Hen looked up into the night, horrified to find herself face-to-face with the massive silhouette of man she now recognized as Cats Vericcio, holding the handle of the outside door to the cellar.

"Henrietta," he said coldly.

CHAPTER TWENTY-NINE

Everyone has heard of the 'fight or flight' response brought forth by pure adrenaline. It's primitive, really. Some animals go on the immediate attack while others run desperately for their lives. This survival instinct is meant to be beneficial for the continued existence of the species. There is a third option, however, that is lesser known. Fight, flight, or *freeze*. For example, a rabbit, helpless to combat or outrun its opponent, might just remain completely and irrevocably still in hopes of tricking the predator into thinking it is already dead. This is, perhaps, the least helpful of the three, and quite unfortunately, the exact response that Hen had to confronting a man she knew to be dangerous, and possibly even murderous.

He had only said her name, nothing more. Then, before she had time to process, he forcefully grasped her wrists and yanked her up out of the cellar. Though he looked to be getting on in years, he was very strong, and Hen was no match for him. He zip-tied her wrists together before she had a second to think. Didn't she learn about how to evade a zip-tie constraint in that self-defense class she took years ago? She couldn't remember. She couldn't think straight. Subconsciously, Hen's eyes darted over to her car. She was so close to escape. Even with her wrists bound together, she could still drive...probably.

"That hunk-of-junk isn't taking you anywhere. We've taken the liberty of slashing your tires for you." Mr. Vericcio's voice was so deep, it shook Hen to the core, like the boom of a firework. Hen's thoughts went to last summer and laying on a blanket in the backyard, watching the municipal fireworks show from the safe distance of a few miles away. Lilly was asleep in her arms, while she enjoyed the comfort of Harry's arms around her. She needed to be strong, she needed to be careful. For her family.

"What exactly do you want?" Hen made eye contact with her aggressor, trying to appear braver than she felt. She was careful not to use his name. Perhaps she could plead ignorance.

"You are the one who needs to answer a few questions, Miss Bellemore," he growled and shoved her back inside the front door of the mansion. *It's Mrs.* she thought indignantly but dared not say aloud. Once inside, he locked the door behind them and practically threw Hen through the front doorway.

Large portraits of what Hen assumed were members of the Nettles family cluttered the walls, though many of them were obscured in darkness. The subjects all seemed miserable. Maybe it was in fashion to have your likeness painted looking as dismal as possible. Or maybe they were just sick of sitting painstakingly still while someone painted their picture. Either way, they were exceptionally depressing. And also exceptionally creepy. Though Hen couldn't make out the details of each portrait, the whites of the eyes seemed to reflect the moonlight creeping through the old thick windows. It was as if endless sets of eyeballs were peering out of the walls, watching her, judging her, perhaps even pitying her, powerless to help. Mr. Vericcio followed her gaze to the paintings.

"How's it feel?" he shouted at the lifeless faces. "You are all dead and here I am, in your godforsaken house." He turned to Hen who he was still clutching tightly. "And they're all dead," he whispered, "so what good is it to them anyway?"

Hen felt a shiver go down her spine, wanting desperately to break free and run but she was frozen, as powerless as the people in the paintings around her. She also had no idea as to what Mr. Vericcio was referring to. *'What good is it to them'... did he mean the house or something else?*

A noise caught her attention and it appeared as if Mr. Vericcio had heard it too. All of a sudden, he seemed to be shifty-eyed and in a hurry. He dragged Hen upstairs, stopping in the hall to listen for a sound. In complete silence, he continued his fastidious search, with Hen in tow, carefully examining each of the upstairs rooms. Hearing nothing, he finally gave up and yanked Hen back downstairs and through a door Hen recognized. He had taken her back into the study.

Hen noticed the passageway had been shut. She truly was trapped. Mr. Vericcio pointed to the velvet chair and shoved Hen toward it. She took a deep breath and sat obediently.

"Why *you*, huh?" he bellowed. "I've never heard of you before. You're a nobody!" Hen nodded. She wasn't sure what else to do.

He continued, "So you end up with these... these *stupid* books! I need to know why." There was a pause, he actually wanted some kind of response this time.

"I don't know. They just showed up at my door," Hen replied, voice wavering.

"Do you think I'm an idiot, Miss Bellemore?"

"I don't know you," Hen heard herself reply. Mr. Vericcio was taken aback a bit by Hen's ability to ignore the question altogether.

"Well, I am *not*," he answered for her. He brushed off the collar of his suit jacket and continued, "but I don't like childish puzzles. Essie always deemed me a complete moron because I didn't want to waste my time with her insipid little puzzles. And here she is, taunting me." He was talking more to himself than to Hen in the latter half of his statement and took a quick pause, then returned his focus back to Hen. "But *you*! You're just like her. You figured out her games, her clues, her...secrets." He clung to the final 's' on 'secrets' like a snake, taunting its prey.

"I really don't think I'm as clever as you seem to think I am," Hen answered softly.

"Then what are you doing here, Henrietta Bellemore? Why were you seen dropping off evidence to convict a certain George Nettles-Brown? Why were you seen bringing in a certain Derrick Tittle to produce a confession to the police? You really do think I'm an idiot!" With each question, his voice rose in volume as he moved closer and closer to Hen, until he was shouting, a foot away from her face.

Hen turned her head down and away, averting her eyes by looking at the desktop in front of her. She caught a glimpse of a framed photograph sitting upon the desk but didn't have time to think much about it because Mr. Vericcio was shouting once more.

"So, what am I to believe then?" he bellowed. Then he leaned down and stared directly into Hen's eyes. "I know that you know." Hen only stared. What did she know? She was pretty sure that she didn't. Then, something came to her.

"We?" she said. Mr. Vericcio continued to appear livid, but also confused. "You said 'we slashed your tires'. Who else is here?" She really just wanted to avoid answering his questions, so she came up with one of her own.

"Yes, Miss Bellemore. It's not just me that's been keeping tabs on you," he said with a smirk. At that very moment, the study doorknob turned and in walked none other than Thad Neilson.

"Thad?" Hen whispered in disbelief.

"I'm sorry, Hen." His eyes fell to the floor.

"I...I-" Hen couldn't form a full sentence, paralyzed with the shock of Thad's betrayal.

"Why did you come here?" Thad murmured, a hint of anger in his voice.

"Do us a favor and leave us alone for a moment." Mr. Vericcio waved his hand at Thad. "We need to get to the bottom of something."

"Sir, I-"

Mr. Vericcio cut Thad off, "Just go." At which point, Thad left quietly, hanging his head. Mr. Vericcio's attention was back to Hen. "So, the question is, are you going to help me Miss Bellemore?"

Hen made eye contact but did not affirm or deny his query.

Mr. Vericcio continued, "I'm going to need an answer from you, because you see, Hen-ri-e-tta," he annunciated every syllable of her name mockingly, "you are a…liability."

Hen felt herself swallow, then spoke calmly, "What do you want exactly?"

"That's the second time you've asked me that question," he gruffly replied, "a question that you certainly know the answer to."

Hen stared blankly back.

"The money!" Mr. Vericcio barked. "Where is it?"

CHAPTER THIRTY

The money? Hen nodded as if she knew. She assumed he was referring to the missing fortune, which, of course, she knew nothing about, but she couldn't let on that she was completely oblivious to its whereabouts. Hen needed to keep herself from being expendable.

Hen chose her words carefully, "I'm not sure that it's here."

"So where then?" Mr. Vericcio bellowed.

"Well…" Hen flipped through the book in front of her, pretending to be looking for something specific. "Here, you see." she pointed to the random page open before her. It just happened to be the poem, Sing a Song of Sixpence. She read aloud the first few stanzas:

Sing a song of sixpence

A pocket full of rye

Four and twenty blackbirds

Baked in a pie

When the pie was opened

The birds began to sing

Wasn't that a dainty dish

To set before the king?

The king was in his counting house

Counting out his money

The queen was in the parlor

Eating bread and honey

"And that means what?" Mr. Vericcio grumbled impatiently.

"Well… um, well…" Hen mumbled, trying desperately to come up with something.

"Spit it out!"

"Well…she drew this little box around 'sixpence' in the first stanza and around 'money' in this stanza here, so…um, that probably means that the money is…in a box…somewhere. Um, perhaps…like her…coffin?" Hen swallowed. She was a terrible liar.

However, it seemed she had been convincing enough to fool her counterpart, at least for the time being. He paced over to the fireplace. "No coffin," he muttered, staring into the cold ashes. "Old Essie was cremated. Just like…" His voice trailed off.

Hen looked up at him, waiting for him to finish his sentence. *Who? Just like who?* In that very moment, something caught her eye once more that ultimately answered that question for her. It was the photograph resting upon Mrs. Nettles' desk, placed in a jeweled frame. A sweet, candid, and slightly goofy close-up shot of her and her husband, whose name Hen couldn't remember. They looked really happy, both dressed up for some fancy occasion, Essie leaning in to kiss her spouse's cheek and him making a funny face. They were young. She wore an off-the-shoulder dress which was most likely considered rather revealing in her day, while he wore a bowtie and a vest with…small, metal buttons, each engraved with the letter F.

Hen remembered now, F for… "Francis," she whispered aloud.

Mr. Vericcio whipped around and stormed toward her. Hen jumped up out of the chair and bolted for the door, but after having her wrists tied so tightly together, she had begun to lose the feeling in her hands and fingers, finding herself lacking in dexterity. She couldn't twist the doorknob and open the door fast enough.

Her aggressor's meaty hand swung around and slammed the door shut. He put his giant frame between Hen and the door, then grabbed her by the shoulders and lifted her to his eye level, her feet dangling.

"You clever, clever cretin," he hissed in her face, his breath rank with cigar smoke. He threw her down to the floor and brushed off his jacket sleeves. "You know what, it feels good to get it off of my chest after all these years. Yes, I killed old Franky. He was stealing Essie away from her career, which meant he was stealing money away from me. He drank too much. He had no drive. He was happy just to live on the coattails of his wife. Pathetic. And here I was, this young man, who had given my whole life to this woman, and she would rather marry an old nobody. She was infuriatingly devoted to that idiot. I hated the man." Mr. Vericcio leaned down a bit, closing in on Hen. "It's a shame he went missing. A real shame that no one found him, or what was left of him in that incinerator. He always did love that dirty old workshop. It's fitting for his final resting place."

"You pushed a helpless old man into an incinerator?" Hen whispered in disbelief.

"Helpless! Ha! You're right, pathetically helpless. And you know what, no one missed him. I took care of him like I took care of all of Essie's problems." He stood back up again and leaned against the door. "Except Essie herself. She missed him."

"You killed her too, didn't you?" Hen heard herself ask.

Mr. Vericcio's demeanor softened a bit as he glanced down at his feet, "Put the old girl out of her misery." He looked back into Hen's eyes. "I had to. I kept waiting on her to just die of old age, but she refused. She became this insufferable busybody. I think she suspected that I had killed Francis for a long time, but she was coming to the end of her life, wanting to tie up loose ends. I knew that she had every intention to expose me. She just wouldn't…let it go. If she only just let herself die…" It was as if he was justifying his actions to Hen. She didn't have any idea what to do, what to say. He had just confessed to her that he murdered two people. As far as Hen knew, she was the only one who knew. There was nothing keeping him from killing her too. Except…

"So now you are looking for the missing money," Hen said frankly.

He was a bit surprised by her directness.

"Yes," he responded, "and you are going to tell me where it is."

Hen took a deep breath and in her most commanding voice replied, "Right. I suppose that is my only option. I don't know exactly where it is, but I do know exactly how to find out." *Please don't realize that's a complete lie.*

"For your sake, Miss Bellemore. I hope you're right."

31

CHAPTER THIRTY-ONE

Hen reached out slowly and pulled the stack of books toward her. Mr. Vericcio kept an intensely close eye on her every little move. She flipped slowly through the pages, tracing the lines with her finger, pretending to be looking for something specific. In actuality, she was just buying herself time.

Mr. Vericcio's massive frame loomed over her, every once in a while, leaning closer to try to see for himself what she was deciphering. Hen would quickly turn the page when she noticed him creeping closer, not wanting to give him the opportunity to realize this hunt for a specific hidden clue was all a hoax. She had no idea where that money was. And not a single hint seemed to jump out at her from these pages.

Her counterpart began fidgeting with impatience, so Hen uttered a few ooh's and hmm's to have him believe that she was onto something. *Something, give me something, Mrs. Nettles,* she pleaded in her head. At a snail's pace, she turned each page, yet all too quickly, Hen was running out of pages, running out of time, and she was no closer to an answer or a plan.

The last page of the last book of the stack lay open before her. What was she going to do? Finally, he'd had enough. Mr. Vericcio slammed the book shut on Hen's fingers which would have hurt even more if she hadn't lost feeling in her hands.

"Well?" he boomed.

Think of something, Hen. Anything. Literally say anything.

"You have no idea, do you?" he grunted angerly.

Anything, Hen.

"Lavender's Blue!" she blurted. "The last verse says, um, something like: if you should die- dilly dilly- as it may hap, you should be buried, um…under the…tap."

Mr. Vericcio stared at her for a long, uncomfortable pause.

"Dilly dilly," Hen said timidly, completing the rhyme.

His expression had changed from simply anger to confusion and anger.

"Dilly dilly?" he bellowed. "And this ridiculous nonsense will tell me where my money is?"

"Uh…yes." Hen nodded, trying to be confident and convincing but failing. He hadn't fallen for this lie.

"Buried underground, huh?" he growled as he grasped her arm tightly and yanked her up. "How convenient. That's exactly where you're going." He pulled her forcefully toward the door.

Hen twisted and squirmed with all she could to break free of his grasp to no avail. In the struggle, her phone fell from her pocket and thudded on the hardwood floor. Mr. Vericcio kicked the phone with the tip of his toe, sending it sliding across the room. Her breath quickened.

"What else are you hiding in your pockets, Miss Bellemore?" he hissed, shoving his large hand into the left back pocket of her pants. She closed her eyes, feeling violated and terrified. "You thief!" he exclaimed, unfolding the scarf. "This might just be useful," he mused, wrapping and tying Hen's ankles tightly together with the silk. "What else is in here, hmm?" His voice sent chills up her spine.

He shoved his hand into her right back pocket. "What have we here?" He held up the charred button to get a closer look, then quickly chucked it across the room and into the fireplace. He grabbed Hen even tighter and pulled her toward him, causing her to lose her balance now that her ankles were bound. "You are here to expose me, aren't you?" His face was inches from hers. "You aren't here for the money at all." Hen felt her body begin to shake in trepidation.

And with that, he dragged her through the dark mansion, through an even darker hallway, and down a winding staircase that was darkest of all. Hen's eyes hadn't adjusted to the lack of light, but she heard distinctly the cranking of a handle and the scrape of a metal door being forced open. He flicked a switch and with a faint zapping sound, a single bulb lit the room.

Hen looked around but said nothing. The room was oddly shaped, triangular, with two small walls and one long one. The floor was poured cement, which along with the cinderblock walls produced a very gray atmosphere. Besides the bulb that hung from the ceiling, there was absolutely nothing in the room, not even a cobweb.

"Empty," Mr. Vericcio grumbled. "The fortune that was supposed to reside here should have been mine."

The room was dry and fairly clean compared to the section of basement that Hen had explored earlier. Perhaps they were farther from the mansion than she had realized. She wasn't sure, having become disoriented as she was dragged through the darkness.

Hen heard footsteps approach down the stairs from behind her, but before she could turn to see who it was, a heavy push heaved her into the room and the metal door slammed shut. She was alone, trapped deep underground, with no way to escape.

Hen lay on the ground, completely quiet and still. She heard muffled voices, soft through the thick door but clear enough to make out.

It was Thad, "So where is she?"

"She was…unwilling to help. I let her go."

Hen shouted toward the closed door, "Thad! Thad!"

He hadn't heard her. "That doesn't seem like her." Thad's voice seemed quieter as if he was walking away.

"Just trust me." Mr. Vericcio's was quieter as well.

"Okay…" Thad's voice trailed off.

With all her might, Hen screamed, "I'm here! In here! Thad! I'm in here!" She waited for a response, anything at all, but to her utter disappointment, she heard nothing. Both men had left her, locked in what was basically a dungeon.

The light that emanated from the single bulb was dim, but her eyes had finally adjusted. Hen skimmed her hands across the surface of the cold, metal door. No handle. The low ceiling was sheet rock. There wasn't a crawl space small enough for a mouse to escape, let alone a grown woman. The three walls seemed to close in on her and Hen found herself feeling woozy. She sat in the center of the room and hugged her knees to her chest, giving herself a moment to let the gravity of her situation wash over her.

As she sobbed, she gave her knees an extra tight squeeze, thinking back to the last hug she gave Lilly before leaving the house that night. *Lilly. What I would do to hug you right now.* Hen wept uncontrollably at the thought. She pulled her feet in even closer, curling into a tiny ball, and as she did, her fingers brushed up against the silky scarf around her ankles.

Feverishly, she began picking at the knot, taking small breaks to shake her hands in attempts to get the blood flowing into her fingertips. After a long and tedious effort, her legs were free! She pulled the scarf to her chest and hugged it, then wiped her damp eyes with the silk.

184

Hen stood up and took a deep and determined breath. *Okay, now to get out of here.*

32

CHAPTER THIRTY-TWO

Hen's first thought was to take a crack at the door. She tried simply pushing it which was useless and extremely tiring. Then, she smartened up, sliding her fingers in the tiny crevice beneath, tracing the nearly airtight joining between the door and its frame. She was looking for a weakness, something that she could work with. Unfortunately, this all proved pointless.

Hen had come to the realization that she was trapped within the very vault that she had read about in the paper, a vault that supposedly had unspoken worth preserved inside. The door in question was built to withstand break-ins, and in her case, break-outs as well.

She needed a change of direction. Hen looked around the room. It was completely empty. Nothing hung on the walls, no furniture within it. *If there really had been money in here, wouldn't there at least be boxes or shelving or something left behind?*

That gave Hen an idea. She got down on her hands and knees and looked for anything that might be laying on the floor, perhaps hiding in the shadowy corners. Her goal was to collect anything, no matter how small, to try to come up with a plan.

Surprisingly, there were a few small objects to speak of, hiding in plain sight. The singular bulb only really lit the center of the room, so the edges were obscured until Hen made her way carefully around, brushing her hands across the ground. She brought all that she found to the center of the room and placed it on the scarf which she had laid out on the floor. She thoughtfully examined her findings in the dim light. Then, she took inventory and, of course, made a list.

1. A rusty coin
2. Three identical screws
3. A piece of dirty, frayed string
4. A handful of rocks (perhaps pieces of cement?)
5. Her wedding ring, which she kept on her finger and didn't place on the floor but still considered as something she could use

Not a lot to work with honestly, Hen thought to herself. *Oh wait...*

6. The scarf itself

The recollection of Mr. Vericcio shoving his massive hand into her pockets as he grabbed out that scarf and the button sent a chill down Hen's spine. Subconsciously, she reached back and touched her pocket at the memory, but in doing so, she realized that there was one thing he didn't take.

Hen pulled out a tiny piece of paper. It was the final map. A series of boxes with two words written on the back: straight-wait.

Straight to where? Wait for what? Hen sat down to ruminate on this discovery. She scooched back a few feet to lean her back against the door. Hen held the paper in front of her, half expecting to see a clue appear when she held it up to the light. No such luck.

As she viewed the hand-drawn map in her hands, an idea popped into her head. *It couldn't be, there's no way,* she thought. Hen counted the boxes on the paper, first horizontally (eighteen) and then vertically (twenty-two). Then she dropped the paper below her field of vision and counted the cinderblocks on the wall in front of her: eighteen wide by twenty-two high. *This has to be a coincidence, right?*

Though she tried to downplay her excitement in her mind, Hen's heart beat a little faster with the spark of hope. Still clutching the paper, Hen walked forward toward the long wall and found the block where the two lines intersected on her map. Now that she was close to it, she immediately noticed that this block seemed to be pushed out just slightly from the others. *What if this is another secret passage?* Hen tried desperately to jiggle the block free. She couldn't push it, but she could almost pull it, if only she could chip away at the mortar a bit.

Hen ran over to her pile of makeshift tools and snatched two of the screws. She painstakingly chipped and scratched at the edges of the cement block until finally, it began to budge. As she carefully pulled it toward herself, she recognized that it was a false block which allowed it to conceal a hidden compartment within the wall itself.

She reached her hand in, hoping for a lever or a handle that would reveal her means of escape. Quite dishearteningly, there was only one object inside. It was not a lever, nor was it a handle. It was just a small wooden box.

Hen pulled the box from its hiding place and shed a few tears. The disappointment of having not discovered another passage was a bitter pill to swallow. She sat back down in the middle of the room and shook her hands. Her fingers were now purple. She should have paid closer attention in self-defense class.

Upon closer inspection, the box was, in fact, a puzzle box. She thought back to her conversation with Derrick at the bakery. He had mentioned a puzzle box that Mrs. Nettles had given him to open, but he was unable to. Hen wondered if it could have been this exact one.

Though Hen found herself no closer to escape, at least she had a distraction: figuring out this box. Hen sat cross-legged and placed the other tiny objects in her lap in order to not lose them, then she used the scarf to wipe off the intricate designs carved into the box.

It was covered with beautiful carvings and as Hen began to mess around with it, she came to realize how complicated it truly was.

Tiny squares slid back and forth along the top, knobs spun along the sides and hinges hinted that the box could fold in on itself if manipulated correctly, though Hen couldn't quite figure that part out yet.

With a million fears she didn't wish to think about bidding to enter her mind, Hen found peace in the puzzle box. Time didn't seem to exist within the vault, but if she were keeping track the minutes (or maybe hours) seemed to pass quickly as she prodded at the tiny mechanisms. Had she been anywhere else, she would have given up, but with nowhere to go and nothing else to do, Hen focused her complete attention on the puzzle. Eventually, she began to figure it out.

The movable squares upon the lid were first. She soon discovered that she could move them left, right, up, or down, but didn't know in which order. It took her embarrassingly long to figure out that the arrows were right in front of her, embossing the scarf that lay upon her lap.

Once the lid had opened, she needed to move the gears on the sides. With time on her side, she attempted just about every configuration possible until the hinge freed itself.

From there, she could fold the box to uncover a tiny door. This part was tricky. She needed six numbers in order to unlock it. At first, she tried 1-1-1-1-1-1, then 1-1-1-1-1-2, and so on and so forth, but at about 1-1-2-4-5, she gave up. *This is impossible.*

Hen took a break from puzzling. The walls were becoming more and more confining. It was then, that the thoughts she had been fighting off began to invade her mind. *Am I going to die in here? Am I ever going to see another person again? I might never see Abby again, or Harry...or Lilly.* Hen burst into tears. *Why did I come here? How could I have been so stupid? Will I never again be able to play airplane with Lilly? Never hear her giggle when I tickle her? Never see her smile when I wake her up in the morning or splash with her in the bath at night? Never read her another story or silly nursery rhyme?* Hen paused her own thoughts and grabbed the piece of paper from her pocket.

'Straight-Wait' it read. *Think nursery rhymes, what nursery rhyme has these words?* Finally, it came to her. Hen had just read it to Abby at the kitchen table. Gosh, that seemed so long ago now.

"One, two, buckle my shoe…" Hen spoke aloud. "Seven, eight, lay them…*straight!*" Hen picked the box up once more and turned the first two knobs to reveal a seven and an eight respectively. She continued to go through the rhyme in her head as she talked through it aloud, "Eleven, twelve, dig and delve… seventeen, eighteen, maids in *wait*-ing!" She changed the next four numbers to one-seven-one-eight.

The box clicked and the door sprung open. The sudden action made Hen jump. She eagerly reached for what was inside: a key; a small, seemingly normal key. Hen held it up to the light. *What good is a key for a door that has no keyhole?* she wondered, but before she could answer that question, heavy footsteps approached. Hen stood up, dropped the key in her pocket and clutched the box to her chest, ready to either fight for her life or make a run for it up the stairs. She didn't know how fast she would be with her tired body and throbbing knee, and she certainly was no match for Mr. Vericcio in terms of brawn, but she had too much to lose to freeze at this chance.

CHAPTER THIRTY-THREE

It seemed to take ages with Hen eagerly awaiting the door to swing open as she listened to the metallic sound of the handle on the other side rattle about. Finally, as if in slow motion, the hinges began to creak and a dark hallway to freedom appeared. The beam of a flashlight crept into the room, blinding her a bit, though she didn't let it stop her. Hen swung with all her might and wacked her assailant square in the face with the wooden box. He fell to the ground and cried out in pain as she clumsily, but with surprising rapidity, climbed the stairs.

"Hold on a sec!" she heard someone yell from the bottom of the staircase. It wasn't Mr. Vericcio's voice, but Thad's calling after her. She didn't obey, she didn't dare stop. Hen made it to the top of the staircase and into a slightly brighter hallway in the mansion. The lights were still off, but the moon's glow streamed in through a large window at the end of the hall.

A terrifying thought struck her as she crept through the mansion. If it was Thad that had opened the door, then Mr. Vericcio was still lurking around somewhere. Hen felt her breath quickening in fear. Should she head straight to the car? Perhaps he was calling her bluff about the tires being slashed. Or maybe she should head to the study and retrieve her phone. Then once she was outside, she could hide and call for help. Hen made the decision to go with the latter.

She tiptoed carefully, feeling as though Mr. Vericcio was about to pop out and grab her at any moment. She walked only on the carpets and not the hard floor to muffle her footsteps. Hen made a few wrong turns before finding her bearings and catching a glimpse of the desk light spilling through the study door. It was open.

Should she risk it? She racked her brain. Had they left the door open earlier? She couldn't remember. There was no sign of movement, no hint of sound coming from the room. She would sneak in, snatch the phone from the floor and bolt out, ready to pivot and run at the slightest sign of Mr. Vericcio. He was older than her, so she could maybe outrun him with adrenaline on her side.

Hen snuck in and looked on the ground where she knew the phone had been. She searched frantically for it but couldn't find her phone anywhere. It was gone! *Okay, Plan B, make my way alone through the woods. Not ideal, but doable.* Hen bolted for the door, but was shocked to see Thad once more, standing in the opening, hand to his temple.

"Get out of here, Thad!" she screamed and ran toward him, aiming to squeeze past.

"Can you just chill for five seconds?" he asked calmly. Hen kicked his shin and tried to make a break for it, but Thad was able to restrain her. "Can't you see, I'm trying to help you!" he grunted, pushing her back into the room. Hen stopped for a moment and looked into his eyes. Something about his expression made her believe he was sincere. She hoped desperately that she was right.

"Where's Mr. Vericcio?" Hen whispered anxiously.

"He got away." Thad sighed, rubbing his leg. "Jesus, right in the shin..."

"Got away? You mean he's gone?" Hen asked, unwilling to trust him.

"Look why don't you just sit for a second and I'll explain, okay? Just don't kick me...or hit me with anymore hard objects, deal?" Hen nodded but thought to herself, *I make no promises.*

Hen sat in a tiny wooden chair, close to the door, so that if she felt threatened at any point, she could run out.

Thad leaned up against the desk and continued, "So, first of all, I should tell you, I've been tailing Cats Vericcio for a while. Essie Nettles knew my dad and when she found out I did a little detective work on the side, she asked me to keep an eye on him."

"Detective work?" Hen inquired.

"Yeah...I don't really work at the post office. I just know Bob and told him I'd watch the place for a minute when I saw you coming. I suggested he go on a smoke break. Bob's actually a terrible employee, nice guy though..." He smiled and shook his head, paused for a moment, then got back to his story. "So anyway, Essie had the notion that Cats had murdered her husband and that he maybe had it out for her as well, though they were friends and I think she hoped she was wrong."

"She was right," Hen affirmed quietly.

"Yeah, I know," Thad said. "So, she started writing down observations about him and a few others that she knew were up to no good. But they weren't just diary entries, she used these little riddles, jotted down into books and things. She wouldn't just spell it out for me, she said I needed to figure it out, like I needed to earn the truth or something. She was a little..."

"Eccentric?" Hen suggested.

"Odd," Thad retorted, "but I liked her anyway and I felt a responsibility to help since she knew my dad and all, so I said I'd look into it. Then, all of a sudden, she died. I know she was old, but I had just seen the woman, and I can tell you, she wasn't on her death bed or anything. It was very much out of the blue."

"Because she was killed."

"Right, and it seemed like I was the only one who believed that. Then, I get instructions from Essie in an unopened envelope from her lawyer telling me to deliver these books and notes to a random address. I almost didn't do it, but when I realized it was *your* house, I decided to follow through. You always were the smartest kid in our class. Maybe you could figure out her puzzles."

"But why didn't you just tell me?"

"I didn't want you to be involved like that. If you didn't know what was going on, you wouldn't be in harm's way. Or so I thought-" he stopped his story suddenly and looked toward Hen's hands. Then, he quickly reached into his pocket and pulled out a multitool. "Oh my gosh, I'm so sorry, here…"

He cut the zip tie around Hen's wrists, and she winced in pain as the blood began to return to her fingers. She gently wrung her hands together and inspected the area where her skin had been rubbed raw from the binding.

"Aw, geez. I'm sorry, Hen. Maybe I did deserve being hit in the face." Hen grinned a bit without looking up at him and Thad continued, "You should know, as soon as he started getting paranoid about you, I tried to keep you away from here. I set a road trap to keep you from getting to the mansion. I even outright told you to stop getting involved in that text."

"But by that point, I was already involved," Hen accused.

"Well, yeah, but that wasn't the plan. My plan was to let you figure out the clues, from a safe distance. Then, in the meantime, I would get close to Cats, let him think I was just some dumb guy looking to get a piece of the fortune should he ever find it. I hoped he would slip up, spill something, but he was very careful. He wouldn't even let me poke around without his watchful eye."

"But he confessed to me. Right here in the study," Hen said.

"That's awesome, but if we had some tangible evidence, that would be even better."

"There's Francis' button around here somewhere, a fancy one from his vest, engraved with an 'F'. It's all charred from the…"

"Incinerator!" Thad shouted, excitedly. "Where is it? Do you have it?"

"No, but it got thrown over here somewhere."

Hen began to lead him over to the fireplace to look for it, when all of a sudden, "Stay away from her!" Tammy jumped out from behind the secret passage and pepper-sprayed Thad in the face.

"Jesus!" he hollered, holding his eyes.

"Tammy!" Hen exclaimed, giving her a big hug. "Where have you been?" Hen looked over sympathetically at Thad as he crouched down in pain. "Also, I think he might be on our side…" she confessed to Tammy.

"Oh, oops. Sorry!" she shrugged.

(34)

CHAPTER THIRTY-FOUR

Hen, Tammy, and Thad made their way down a long hall and turned into a wide-open room, flicking on the lights. The women sat at a long counter to regroup in what Hen now realized was the butler's kitchen while Thad shoved his face under the running tap, grumbling under his breath.

Tammy glanced over at him, "I really am sorry about that." She peeked at Hen, raising her eyebrows, shrugging her shoulders, and making a 'whoops' face. Hen did what she could to keep from chuckling.

"It's...fine," Thad responded, gritting his teeth, head still under the running water in the kitchen sink.

Hen was too curious to wait any longer and quickly changed the subject, asking "So Tammy, where were you? What happened?"

"Where were *you*, girl?" she replied. "I was so worried about you!"

"Me? What do you mean?"

"Well, I thought that we were supposed to meet outside the mansion," Tammy explained, "so I parked my aunt's car off to the side of the road before I reached that creepy driveway. I was pretty early though because I was all amped up to be a spy again, so all I could do was chill in the car and wait. I couldn't even listen to music because her radio is broken. Oh yeah, and I had picked up an extra-large soda on my way over. But then, with nothing else to do, I ended up drinking the whole darn thing in like two minutes. Well, that was a mistake. There aren't any freaking bathrooms in the woods. I couldn't help it, I had to go, so I walked really far from the road so no one would see and…" she leaned toward Hen and whispered, "I peed in the woods. For like ten minutes, seriously."

"We've all done it," Thad chimed in from the sink.

"Shut up, Thad!" both girls hollered over.

Hen turned back to her friend, "Okay, so then what?"

"Well, it took me a little time to find my way back to the car. I had gone kind of far into the woods and forgot how to get back for a minute. The trees all kind of look the same in the dark, you know? But, anyway, I finally found my way back and I noticed a missed call from you. I was such a dummy to leave my phone in the car! I guess I didn't think my little bathroom break would take so long."

"Yeah, I saw it ringing in the car, but it was locked," Hen said.

"Well, yeah. You always need to lock your car, girl." Tammy gave Hen a look. Then she continued, "So anyway, I decided to grab my backpack and walk up the driveway so I didn't announce my presence to everyone." If only Hen had thought to do that. Tammy kept going, "Well, then I see a minivan parked up near the house. No offense, but I feel like a fancy person who is living in a mansion probably doesn't drive a minivan, so I figured it was yours."

Hen smiled, "No offense taken."

"But you left your doors unlocked!" Tammy scolded.

"I did?" Hen asked.

"Yeah. Someone could just reach in and steal something…" Tammy dangled the pepper spray up in the air. *Oh my gosh!* Hen smacked her forehead realizing it was her own pepper spray that

Tammy had attacked Thad with. *Man, I wish I would have had that on me earlier.*

Hen grinned and shrugged, allowing Tammy to continue, "Anyway, after I stole the pepper spray from your purse, I realized that your tires were all slashed." *Oh crap, so Mr. Vericcio really wasn't bluffing.* "So then, I was worried about you a little bit because you didn't have any way of protecting yourself *and* you didn't have any way of leaving." Hen sighed, shaking her head. Tammy, noticing Hen's embarrassment, put her hand on her shoulder and said gently, "It's okay, though. You were nervous."

Hen nodded and smiled, then asked, "Did you run into anyone else?"

"I didn't face-to-face, but I heard this big scary guy talking to this other guy" she gestured to Thad, "about getting rid of an intruder. I was pretty sure they hadn't seen me, so I knew they must be talking about you."

"Probably," Hen said, glaring at Thad.

"I just thought he meant getting you out of the mansion!" Thad pleaded, "I didn't know he was planning to get violent."

Hen and Tammy both looked at Thad, who now was very disheveled, very wet, and very pink in the face.

"Here's the thing," he defended, "as soon as I realized that Cats had taken you, messed with you at all, I laid it all out for him. I played hardball, telling him who I was and all that I knew. But he told me that you were probably running out of air in that vault and if I didn't let you out, you might not make it, so I went down there and was greeted with a blow to the face." Thad sighed, "And then he got away." Hen felt just the littlest bit of guilt for hitting him. The littlest bit.

"But it was worth it to save this girl here, right?" Tammy chimed in.

Thad smiled for the first time since Tammy's arrival. "Yeah," he said kindly.

Still curious, Hen turned to Tammy, "So, why didn't you ask for help?"

"Oh, I did!" Tammy replied, "But, I didn't want you to be sent to jail for breaking and entering, which meant I couldn't call the police. But I did call your friend, Abby. She must have texted me like four billion times."

Hen laughed a bit, "Yeah, that sounds like her."

"And I called a tow truck for your car," Tammy said, "It was this really nice guy, he knows you, I think. I was on the phone with him for a while."

Hen nodded, knowing exactly who she was talking about.

Tammy kept going with her story, "Well, I didn't have any service inside which meant I had to sneak out to make these calls. I crept into the woods so the men I heard inside wouldn't see me or hear me. And then, when I made my way back to the mansion, the front door was locked. But there was another door open! It was a staircase into the cellar. Obviously, I had to see where it led. Hen, you're not going to believe this, I found a-"

"Secret passage," Hen finished her sentence.

"Yeah! You found it too?" Tammy asked.

"I tried to lift the fire poker, which was actually a lever, and it opened up," Hen explained.

"Way cool!" Tammy exclaimed. "So yeah, I must have come from the other way, and the passage door was already open, but the desk light was on, like someone had been in there recently. That's when I was brilliant…" she paused for dramatic effect.

Thad, now joining them at the counter, impatiently asked, "What do you mean, you were brilliant?"

"I set up a camera in the study!" Tammy blurted out. "I may have studied up on sneaky, pervy little electronics so that I could keep my eyes peeled for such things. Also, I bought one online, so I could learn more about it. Unfortunately, Mr. Scary Guy must have taken you to that vault room instead. But wouldn't that have been so awesome if I'd caught the bad guy with my stealth skills?"

Hen and Thad looked at each other in amazement.

Hen spoke up, "Tammy, you *are* brilliant."

"Holy crap, you caught his confession on tape," Thad replied in disbelief.

"Oh my god, really?" Tammy squealed. "Wait, what confession?"

"Where's that camera?" Hen asked.

"I'll show you!" Tammy hopped up and excitedly led the two others to the study.

In a small crevice, hidden amongst the knickknacks on a shelf, Tammy pulled out a tiny box.

"This is it!" she explained proudly.

"So how do we see what's on it?" Thad asked impatiently.

"Here, give me your phone," she instructed Hen, who shrugged, overturning her hands to show that she didn't have one.

"Oh, here." Thad handed Hen her phone, now displaying a large crack across the screen.

Tammy looked at Hen's cracked screen and replied cheerfully, "That's okay. We can use mine. But I don't know if it will work in here. Let's go outside." Then she eagerly led the group through the front door of the mansion and into the fresh air.

The sky was pink with morning light. Hen wasn't sure how much time had passed since she had arrived at the mansion, how long she had crept around the dark hallways, how many minutes or hours she had spent in that vault, but no matter how long it had been, walking out into the sun's morning glow was immediately reassuring. Another day was dawning, in more ways than one.

Sitting on the front step, Tammy dug through her backpack for a USB cord and hooked up her phone to the tiny device. Before long, she had a video cued up on her phone's screen.

As Tammy fast-forwarded a bit, and was about to press play, a big dirty truck came chugging up the driveway. Before Hen had a chance to think about who might be driving it, she was drawn in by a deep voice coming from the video on Tammy's phone, "You clever, clever cretin. You know what, it feels good to get it off of my chest after all these years. Yes, I killed old Franky. He was stealing Essie aw-" Tammy pressed pause and was looking worriedly at Hen.

Thad held his hand to his forehead in disbelief, "Holy sh-"

"You okay, Hen?" Tammy cut him off.

Hen was visually upset with having relived one of the scariest moments of her life, and simultaneously elated at the realization that they had real evidence to convict Cats.

"Yeah, I'm okay," Hen whispered, looking down at her raw wrists.

"If only we knew where he was," Thad said.

"Oh, he's on his way to the station," a familiar voice chimed in. Hen glanced up. It was Derrick.

"Derrick?" Hen asked in sheer surprise. "What on earth are you doing here?"

"Someone gave my cousin a call," he said, gesturing behind him.

Gene appeared, climbing out of his old tow truck parked in the driveway, "Yeah, nice lady called for a tow...in the gosh-darn middle of the night! I woulda' just said wait 'til mornin' but she wouldn't have it. Kinda bossy that one, and chatty too. Told me the whole story."

"What do you mean, he's going to the station?" Thad asked.

Gene answered, "Well, when I got the call from that young lady and told old Derry here, he got in touch with his police buddy and I met 'em at the shop. We may have set up a little road trap in case he tried to get away. Don't know where I got that idea." Gene winked at Hen. "And wouldn't 'ya know it, he done got a flat tire."

"So, my friend, Bill, met up with Cats Vericcio and offered him a ride…" Derrick explained, "to the police station." He looked at his watch, "They are probably already there. I'm sure Bill will be interested in that video that you have there."

"His fancy classic car's blocking that goat path of a road, but I'll get it out of there on the way back," Gene said.

Hen felt the paralyzing tension in her body relax. She let out a heavy, audible sigh of relief.

"So, what do 'ya say *Mrs.* Bellemore? Need a ride?" Gene inquired.

"Yes, please." Hen smiled through happy tears. "That would be wonderful."

CHAPTER THIRTY-FIVE

Hen was more than ready to leave the Nettles Mansion. She walked Tammy down the long driveway and to her car while Gene and Derrick followed slowly behind in Gene's beat-up truck. They decided to come back for Hen's minivan later, opting instead to use the towing equipment to move Cats' car which was currently blocking the road.

Tammy paused and turned to her friend before opening her driver's side door. "Hey Hen?"

"Yeah?" Hen answered.

"Thanks."

"For what? You literally saved the day!" Hen replied.

"Yeah, I did, huh?" Tammy beamed with pride, "But, what I mean is, thank you, for... you know... changing my life... for the better, of course." Hen was taken aback a bit. She hadn't really considered herself capable to change someone's life. It felt good though. The friends exchanged a big hug.

"So, what's next?" Hen asked her friend.

"I don't know, maybe I'll design some chic yet practical spy-wear...since now I'm such an expert and everything." The girls both laughed, then Tammy sighed, "But for real, I need to find another job."

"Maybe you could go to school to study fashion," Hen suggested.

"If I find anyone willing to give me a scholarship, I'd love to!" Tammy replied. "In the meantime though, maybe I'll work at a tech store or something."

"There you go," Hen said.

"You comin'?" Gene's voice called from the truck. Tammy settled in her car and Hen closed the door for her, then walked over to the tow truck and climbed in.

"This shouldn't take too long," Gene assured Derrick and Hen as they made their way down the winding road. As they started on their way, Hen took a moment to appreciate the fact that the two men had seemed to reconcile their differences. Perhaps, in some small way, she had played a part in restoring their friendship. The notion brought a smile to her face.

Hen stared out the window, admiring the shadows of the leaves dancing upon the forest floor. She welcomed the peacefulness of early morning, with the wind blowing gently and the sun's rays beginning to cover the landscape in gold. It seemed as if they were the only living beings awake on that quiet drive through the forest.

That was, however, until they got closer to Cats' car and got a glimpse of the other side of the blocked road. Hen couldn't believe her eyes. A huge crowd was gathered right there on the tiny winding path in the middle of the forest. As the tow truck approached, the horde began to buzz with anticipation. All these people were there to see…her?

Men and women in uniform- policemen, firefighters, even construction workers- were present, most of them put to work corralling the herd. Plenty of people that Hen recognized and even more that she didn't were congregating right there in the road first thing in the morning. A coffee stand had even set up shop to serve the crowd. Before she knew what was happening, reporters came running over, cameras at the ready. A pit formed in Hen's stomach. *Oh geez, I hope Harry doesn't find out about all this on the news.*

"What happened at the mansion, Mrs. Bellemore?" "Were you involved with the nefarious activity surrounding Essie Nettles' death?" "Any sign of the missing fortune?"

Hen was immediately overwhelmed and felt her cheeks getting flushed. Derrick quickly came to the rescue, eloquently responding to questions from the press without really answering anything. Gene got to work hitching up the broken-down car while Hen remained in the passenger's seat, safely distanced from the commotion. She shook her head in amazement. *Where did all these people come from? Were they here when Cats was arrested? How else could they have known about the goings-on with Mrs. Nettles and the mansion?*

Hen rubbed her sore knee and pulled out her phone to distract her. Notifications of about a million missed texts and calls flashed upon the cracked screen. *Of course…Abby.*

Hen finally gave her friend a call back.

Abby's voice on the other end nearly broke her eardrum, "HEN! Oh my god! Are you okay? Where are you? What happened? What's going on? It's freaking morning! Why didn't you call me? Wait, tell me where you are!"

"I'm okay. I'm on my way home," Hen said calmly.

"What happened? How far away are you? Tell me everything."

"I will if you let me get a word in," Hen replied. "As for what happened, um, a lot. I'll fill you in when I get home. I am safe, though. I couldn't call you because I didn't have service, and then I…uh, lost…my phone, but I have it back now. It'll still be a little while before I get home, but I'm on my way. I had to get a ride."

"What happened to your van? Wait, you're getting a ride? With Tammy? Do we really trust her? She called me and said you were in danger last I talked to her and then she never called me back. Maybe I should just come get you." Abby still sounded frantic.

"No, it's okay, really. And don't be mad at Tammy. She kind of saved the day, actually. I'll be on my way as soon as they clear the road. It seems *somebody* called the police, the fire department, the press, and just about everyone else in town," Hen accused.

"Okay, stop raising your eyebrows at me," Abby said. Hen checked the mirror to see if she was raising her eyebrows. She was. "I was just worried. Also, I didn't call the press. People in this town are all too nosy for their own good."

Hen shrugged in agreement, "Well, they're all here now."

"That settles it, guess you're a local celebrity. I knew you first!" Abby teased. "But seriously, can you just fill me in on what actually happened?"

"I will. I promise," Hen assured her, then after a pause, "Hey Abby?"

"She's still asleep. I never left her side," Abby answered without Hen even having to ask.

"Okay." Hen felt happy tears of relief streaming down her face. "See you soon."

"See you soon," Abby responded warmly and hung up.

Hen got out of the passenger's side door and walked past Derrick appeasing the press and Gene pleading with the crowd as they both tried to calmly get the horde of people out of the way.

Hen made her way to the front of the group and stood, head held high, as she announced, "Good morning, everyone. Thank you for taking an interest in what has been going on at the Nettles Mansion. We will be more than glad to answer your questions at a later date.

But for now, please step aside to make way for the tow truck to get through. Thank you."

To her complete surprise, the crowd obeyed. The three reentered the truck and were on their way.

Derrick turned to her. "Nice one, Hen," he acknowledged.

Hen smiled. "I've got a baby to get home to."

The rest of the drive was uneventful, Gene and Derrick talked about this and that while bluegrass music faded in and out on the radio. Hen stared out the window as memories flooded her mind, not of her altercations with Mr. Vericcio or last night's terrifying escapades in the Nettles Mansion but rather of her own life, and more specifically, her life as a mom.

She remembered acting like a bird with Lilly at the park, running through the grocery store pretending that they had won first prize in the buggy race, covering her kitchen in flour as she and Lilly baked cookies. Faced with the fear of her life being over, she realized that being Lilly's mom was what she would miss most about it.

As the roads became more familiar, Hen's heartbeat quickened in anticipation. Never before was she so excited to get home. As the truck slowed, Hen had to stop herself from jumping out before Gene put it in park.

She scrambled down and started to run to the front door, when Derrick spoke up, "Oh, wait! Is this yours?" He held up the puzzle box that Hen had found hidden in the vault.

"You can have it!" Hen called back and bolted to the porch. Abby swung the door open and nearly tackled her with a hug.

"Thanks for everything," Hen said to Abby, doing everything she could to stop herself from running inside.

"Oh, go ahead. We'll talk later," Abby said with a smile.

"Thank you!" Hen answered, already halfway down the hallway.

Hen made her way to the end of the hall, gently opened the door, and walked into the room. Tears poured down her face as she peered over the side of the crib at the most beautiful thing in the whole wide world.

"Mommy!"

CHAPTER THIRTY-SIX

A few weeks later

"That is absolutely insane!" Harry exclaimed, wide-eyed at the kitchen table. Hen had been filling him in on everything that had taken place in his absence since he arrived back home. At first, he was furious and hurt that Hen had kept so much from him, but now he seemed more entranced with the story than anything else. He was constantly, and slightly annoyingly, asking her questions at all times throughout the day. "So he just laid it all out to you, confessing to two murders? That's so stupid! Why would he do that?" Hen shuddered a bit, having an answer but not saying it aloud. Harry quickly caught on. "Because he didn't expect you to be alive to be able to tell anyone else..." he muttered under his breath, clutching his fists.

"Hey!" Hen swiftly changed the subject. "Let's go to that park that Lilly and I found while you were away. It's so beautiful there, I think you'd love it. We can even bring that kite that you bought for Lilly. It's supposed to be a really nice day!"

Harry smiled warmly and put his arm around his wife. "I'd love that." Hen rested her head on his shoulder and took a sip of the coffee that he'd made for her. Hen appreciated the moment. *Mmm, cuddles and hot coffee.*

"But one thing, okay?" Harry continued, his voice soft, "No more secrets, alright? Especially if something exciting happens. I really do want to know."

Hen took a deep breath and nodded. "Deal," she agreed, "and that goes both ways."

"Ah yes, queen." Harry replied, bowing with a flourish. "Lavender's blue, dilly dilly, lavender's gr-" he began to sing loudly in a giddy voice.

"Shh!" Hen interrupted, "You're going to wake the princess!"

"What better way to be woken up than through song!" Harry countered back in a silly voice. "When I am king, dilly dilly" he continued even louder, Hen chasing him around the kitchen.

Out of the blue, there was a knock at the door.

"Why don't you go get Lilly up, I'll get this," Hen suggested. Harry nodded and headed back to the nursery while Hen went to answer the door. It was Derrick and another man that Hen didn't recognize, both of them dressed to the nines. Hen took a quick look down at her outfit for the day: leggings and a too-big, comfy sweatshirt that she got from her mom last Christmas that read, "Moms, we get the job done." *He couldn't have dropped by yesterday when I was wearing my cute yellow dress and had actually showered.*

"Um, hey Derrick," Hen greeted him, unable to hide her confusion as to why he was on her doorstep in the early morning.

"Good morning, Hen!" He was exceptionally chipper.

After an awkward pause, Derrick chimed in again, "Oh, yes! This is Baxter Styles."

Another long pause.

"Hi…" Hen said finally. Baxter was silent.

"He's an attorney," Derrick said quickly, as if that was any explanation as to why he was on Hen's porch.

Hen, still highly confused, whispered, "Derrick, am I in some sort of trouble?" to which, Derrick laughed. Baxter just stood there. *A bit of a wet paper bag, that one,* Hen thought to herself.

"No, Hen. You're not in trouble. I wanted to ask you a few questions in the presence of Baxter here. Do you have a minute?"

"Um, yeah, sure. A minute," Hen agreed. "You guys can sit here if you'd like." The three took a seat on Hen's porch and anxiously awaited what the other was about to say.

Derrick broke the silence, "So Hen, you handed me something in the car when we dropped you off after having left Nettles Mansion. What was it?"

"You mean the puzzle box?" Hen asked.

"Did you get that down, Baxter?" Derrick asked. Baxter nodded. *Maybe he just doesn't talk... ever?* Derrick continued, "And what did it look like, Hen?"

"Don't you still have it?" Hen inquired.

"I do, but trust the process for a moment." Derrick replied.

"Okay, um, it was all made of wood. Intricately carved..." Hen went on to describe every little detail of the object. She was pretty amazed at how accurately she could describe it, but she did spend hours fiddling with it.

When she was finished, Baxter took notes while Derrick went on, "And Hen, where did you find the box?"

Hen's body language became more closed off as she wrapped her arms around herself. She hated reliving that night. It was the same reason that she didn't care to answer during Harry's constant questioning, though she did anyway. Derrick noticed this immediately and gave her a sympathetic look, as if to say, "Just trust me."

"Um, I was…forced…into a small room underground, below the mansion. I have reason to believe that it was a vault."

Derrick interjected, "It was indeed the vault, Thad Neilson will verify that." He gestured to Hen, "Go on, Hen."

"Uh, yeah. So, this is going to sound crazy, but the puzzle box was hidden in the wall. I found it in a compartment behind a false brick."

There was another long pause. Derrick nodded excitedly. Baxter showed no emotion. Hen glanced back in forth between the two of them, not sure why they were asking her these questions.

Derrick took a deep breath and turned his body to face Hen fully, "Hen," he was very serious now, "this is the most important part. Was there anything in the box?"

Hen was sure he would be disappointed. "Yeah. But don't get too excited. It was just a key. I don't even know what it's for."

Derrick literally leapt up out of his chair and shouted, "I told you, Baxter! I knew it!" Even Baxter cracked a smile.

"What?" Hen asked impatiently. "You knew what?"

Derrick took a deep breath to calm himself down a bit. Hen had never seen him so excited. From what she knew of Derrick, he wasn't usually one to show such enthusiastic displays of emotion. He handed her a piece of crisp white paper, which seemed to be a scan from a much older piece of paper.

Hen recognized the loopy handwriting, but it was full of legal jargon which made it hard for her to read.

"What am I looking at?" she asked.

"It's an addendum to Essie Nettles will," Derrick explained. "The puzzle box. It had a false bottom. The paper scanned here was stashed inside." He paused and added, "It's been verified." He pointed to the paragraph near the bottom of the page.

So whoever finds the hidden key has proven to me to possess both patience and cleverness, two traits which I greatly admire. This individual has proven themselves worthy of the material goods found within the safety deposit box unlocked by the key in question.

The remainder of the page went on to describe exactly where that safety deposit box was and how to go about opening it.

Hen wasn't sure what to say or think. She was completely overwhelmed. She went back inside and reached into her purse, grabbing out the key that had fallen to the bottom of the bag, sitting right next to a bobby pin and a stick of gum. Hen walked back outside holding up the key to show the two men. Derrick jumped up again, unable to contain his excitement.

Baxter stood up calmly and walked over to Hen. He then shook her hand and said, "Congratulations, Mrs. Bellemore. It seems that you are entitled to what we believe to be the missing Nettles fortune."

Hen stood like a statue, shaking her head in acknowledgement, but paralyzed otherwise. Now it was her turn to be speechless.

"Well, I'll just let that sink in," Derrick said with a wide, white grin plastered upon his face. "And we can double-check what's actually in that safety deposit box whenever you are…" he glanced at Hen who was still frozen in astonishment, "uh, ready." Both men left the porch and Hen still hadn't moved. In fact, she was bumped from behind with the door when Harry walked out onto the porch, Lilly in his arms.

"What was that about?" Harry asked nonchalantly.

Hen blinked, then came-to a bit. She turned slowly and faced her husband and her beautiful little daughter. Hen reached over and held Lilly in her own arms, giving her an extra big hug.

A smile slowly crept over Hen's face. "Remember when you said I should tell you right away when something exciting happens…"

"Yeah…" Harry patiently replied, though he was eager to hear her continue.

"Well, you know that key I found?"

Harry nodded.

"Um, well, I found out what it unlocks."

"Oh cool! What is it?" Harry asked.

"We still have to verify it, but it might be the key to…the missing fortune."

Harry stood completely aghast.

Hen laughed, "Yeah that's how I feel too. I'm not really sure what to even do with that kind of money."

"Please share!" Lilly chimed in.

Hen gave her another big hug, "You sweet girl. I love that idea."

Harry grinned at his wife in admiration. "You're a great mom, you know." Hen's heart melted at the remark. Harry turned to go back inside. "Hey, I'll grab Lilly's jacket and we can go if you're ready." *It was nice to have him home.*

"Ready, Lilly?" Hen began to reach for her daughter's tiny hand to walk her to the car, but Lilly's interest was drawn elsewhere. She toddled as fast as her little feet would take her toward the oversized ceramic heron who, to Hen's chagrin, remained in her front garden.

As Hen drew near to her least favorite lawn decoration, she noticed a strange addition. A piece of tattered paper had been speared upon the heron's ceramic beak. *What's this?* Hen questioned to herself.

Setting herself down in the grass with Lilly on her lap, she began to read:

Henrietta, or Hen as I have been told you prefer,

I hope you do not find this request and its means of transference (via heron beak) too impertinent. I was told that you may be able to help me. You see, an old bird I once knew had faith in you. So much so that she wrote to me, in her coded way, to inform me as such. She has since flown the coop, so to speak, as you most assuredly know. The tales of your faithfulness to my lost friend give me the grounds to ask for your assistance now. I fear I may be in danger. Please await my pigeon post.

Sincerely,
Your not-yet-dead friend of a feather

Just as Hen finished reading, Harry popped his head out the front door. Hen nearly jumped out of her skin at the abrupt sound of the door swinging open.

"Didn't mean to scare you," he said with a laugh. "You didn't make it very far." Harry gestured to his wife sitting on the grass a foot off the porch. "What's that?" He was staring at the punctured paper held tight in Hen's hands.

"Oh, um, nothing," she replied quickly. "Grocery list," she added, scooping up Lilly and making her way toward the car with Harry close behind.

"Good idea. Can you add bananas? We're out."

"Sure." Hen flashed him a smile. *And maybe a security camera...*